THE PEDDLER'S WIDOW

Victorian Romance

FAYE GODWIN

PERSONAL WORD FROM THE AUTHOR

Dearest Readers,

I'm so delighted that you have chosen one of my books to read. I am proud to be a part of the team of writers at Tica House Publishing. Our goal is to inspire, entertain, and give you many hours of reading pleasure. Your kind words and loving readership are deeply appreciated.

I would like to personally invite you to sign up for updates and to become part of our **Exclusive Reader Club**—it's completely Free to Join! I'd love to welcome you!

Much love,

Faye Godwin

CLICK HERE to Join our Reader's Club and to Receive Tica House Updates!

https://victorian.subscribemenow.com/

CONTENTS

PART I

CHAPTER 1

DAISY PARKER ROCKED her child in her arms, gazing down at the eyes that were as grey as the sea. There was something mystical about those eyes, especially now. Sleepy and unfocused, they gazed vaguely up at Daisy, a whimsical smile lingering on the child's broad, thin-lipped mouth. It was Bart's mouth, but Daisy had no idea where her daughter had inherited those enchanting eyes. Bart's mother had had amber eyes, like him, God rest her precious soul. And Daisy had never known either of her parents, but her eyes were blue.

She kissed the smooth little forehead, velvet-soft against her lips, and rocked the baby in her arms for a few moments more as she sang the last few notes of the lullaby.

"And if that horse and cart turn around," she sang softly, "you'll still be the sweetest little babe in town."

Fannie's eyes fluttered closed, and Daisy went on rocking her, humming the lullaby's tune until the baby's breathing grew slow and deep with sleep. Slowly, she lowered Fannie into her small crib and tucked her blanket around her.

Straightening, Daisy paused for a moment to gaze out of the window overlooking the street below. It was raining softly outside, a thin mist of grey descending upon the brick buildings that towered on either side of the narrow street. Daisy could see little other than the wall opposite; like her own building, it was featureless but for small square windows at regular intervals.

But the building across the street had more boarded-up windows than glass ones, and Daisy could see small pieces of paper and fabric fluttering from the holes in the walls. The very sight was desolate, making her shudder to the core. She was relieved to turn away from the window and attend to the coal stove in the corner of the room. Her tenement wasn't much, it was true; there was only one room, and the lavatory was all the way downstairs and outside. This room consisted of a bucket for washing, a crib for the baby, a bed with a straw mattress for Bart and Daisy, and a tiny kitchen in the far corner. A large chest served as the pantry, and there was a table just big enough for the two of them, with a highchair for Fannie.

It wasn't much, as Bart constantly reminded her. But just as she constantly told him, after a childhood spent in the workhouse, it was enough for Daisy.

She was cutting and peeling potatoes for dinner when she heard the familiar rumble of the handcart in the street outside, and her heart leaped with an even more familiar excitement. It was a little miraculous that she could pick out the sound of the handcart among the pandemonium of the city in the evening. There was such a rush of people moving along the street below that the sheer sound of their footsteps was already a cacophony; added to that was the rattle of cart wheels, the clop of hooves, the yelling of voices, the shrill clanging sound of a policeman's bell – but among all this, it was nothing for Daisy to identify that quiet rumbling. It was the sound she waited for all day, every day.

She listened to the rest of the sounds that made up the crescendo of her day's symphony: the creak of the front door, the rattle as Bart stowed his handcart in the courtyard, the sound of his footsteps on the stairs, then the creak of their own door as he reached them. Turning around, Daisy held out her arms with a soft cry of delight. "Bart!"

He stepped into the tenement, and immediately the world seemed to be a thousand times more colourful. Bart's skin glowed a healthy tan; his grin sparkled, the greatest jewel in Daisy's world. His brown hair was thinning a little, but it still fell across his forehead in a bouncing wave from underneath his cap, and his warm amber eyes were soft.

"Hello, pet," he said.

Daisy stepped into his embrace, tucking her nose against his throat, smelling his own unique perfume that no one else in the world could equal. He was a little sweaty, to be sure, and there was something of the grime of the city upon him. But something else, too; something essentially Bart, impossible to describe and still more impossible to resist.

She held him for a few long moments before he gently pried her arms away. "Is she asleep?" he asked quietly, his words rumbling in his chest as she leaned against him.

"Yes. But she'll wake up soon, and be so happy to see her papa," said Daisy. She smiled up at him, her hands wrapped in his. "How did it go today, my love?"

"Very well." Bart's smile widened. "It was a good day to be a peddler. Plenty of those small knives went, and I sold that big cast-iron pan, too."

"Ah, Bart. That's wonderful news. But I was asking about the headache you had this morning." Daisy touched his forehead. "You're feeling a little warm."

"Don't worry about that, my love. Just be happy about the money." Bart kissed her cheek. "It means we're one step closer to that shop I promised I'd open someday, and the better home I'll give you both."

Daisy reached up with a smile, touching Bart's smooth cheek. "As long as we can all be together, I don't care where we live. This is enough for me."

"But I want to give you the world, my pet," said Bart.

"You already did," said Daisy softly, "when you spotted me working for that dreadful old Madame Crawley, and asked me to marry you, and refused to stop until I agreed."

Bart chuckled. "Now, Mrs. Parker," he said playfully, "I think you deserve still more than that."

This time, when he kissed her, it was right on the lips, and he kissed her until she was breathless, and then he kissed her some more.

FANNIE'S STEPS were small and wobbly at times, but Daisy still couldn't get used to the fact that her little girl could move so quickly. She clung to Daisy's hand with a small, pudgy fist, almost running along the pavement as she towed Daisy along behind.

"Steady, poppet," Daisy laughed.

"Mama, bird," Fannie cried, pointing.

There was a disillusioned-looking seagull sitting on the low wall that surrounded their tenement building on the street corner. They were still half a block away, and Daisy was impressed that Fannie had been able to spot the seagull at all. Then again, Fannie had always been obsessed with birds.

"Mama, bird," she repeated, tugging harder at Daisy's arm.

"Yes, that's a bird," said Daisy.

"Mama, catch bird," Fannie insisted.

"No, no, poppet. We can't catch the bird. He's too quick."

Fannie snorted. "Bird," she said again sharply.

Daisy couldn't help laughing as Fannie pushed on through a group of old nuns shuffling down the street. "Sorry," she called out to them, nuns scattering in all directions. Fannie didn't seem to notice their existence. Her eyes were fixed on the seagull.

The gull, of course, spotted them when Fannie was still several yards away. With an angry squawk, it unfurled its wings and flapped off, scattering feathers.

"Bird," Fannie wailed, stopping. She stretched out her free hand toward the gull as it soared off into the grey sky. "Bird come back."

"Sorry, poppet. Bird doesn't want to play today." Daisy reached out a hand and a small, white feather landed gently on her palm. She closed her fingers over it.

"Bird," cried Fannie, the edge of a tantrum in her voice.

"No, no. Don't cry. Look." Daisy crouched down in front of Fannie, setting her shopping basket down on the pavement beside her. "Bird left you a present."

"Present?" Fannie's beautiful eyes widened.

"Yes, something just for you. Are you ready?"

Fannie's eyes were dry. She held out her hands, nodding solemnly, and Daisy cupped her hands over Fannie's, feeling the tiny touch of the feather transfer from her palm to her daughter's. At the sensation, Fannie's eyes widened still more.

"Careful, now," said Daisy. "Don't let the wind blow it away." She withdrew her hands, and Fannie carefully cupped her hands around the pure white feather, staring down at it in awe.

"What, Mama?" the child asked in her tiny voice.

"It's a feather, poppet."

"Feav-ver." Fannie stumbled over the *th* sound. "Feavver."

"That's right." Daisy laughed. "Feather."

That familiar rumble reached her ears, and Daisy got up quickly, grabbing her basket. A dart of fear flew through her stomach. It was barely two o' clock in the afternoon, the usual time she took Fannie out for her walk and went to the market. Bart never came home before five.

She turned, and he was coming down the street toward them, towing his handcart, his feet moving in small, shuffling paces as though his bones themselves were aching. One glance told her everything she needed to know: the redness around his eyes, the pallor of his cheeks, the thin sheen of sweat on his brow.

Daisy's blood felt as though it was drenched with cold. She scooped Fannie into her arms and ran toward him, her heart beating frantically in all the wrong places. "Bart? Oh – Bart!"

"It's all right, pet," Bart said as she reached him, but his breathing was harsh and ragged as he dragged the cart behind him. "Don't fuss, now."

"Darling, you're – " Daisy touched his brow, and found it nearly burned her with its heat. "You're sick."

"Papa," Fannie held out her arms to him.

"It's all right. It's just a touch of the cold, that's all," said Bart, slowly, but his teeth were gritted in pain. He managed a faint smile for Fannie.

"Here. Give me the cart. Go up to bed." Daisy didn't know much about sickness, but she knew this was no cold.

"No, no. I'll help you," said Bart. "Open the gate."

Daisy hurried on ahead, pulling wide the gate that led into the courtyard where Bart kept his cart, and he stumbled forward.

"Papa, bird present." Fannie held out her hand, showing him the white feather. "Feavver."

"Very nice, pet," murmured Bart, hauling the cart inside.

Daisy swung the gate shut. "Now, please, darling," she said. "Come up to bed, and I'll run and fetch the doctor, and – Bart!"

Her husband had crumpled over and fallen to the ground, where he lay motionless.

"Papa sleep," said Fannie.

Daisy put the child down and ran to him, crouching beside him. "Bart. Bart!" she cried, shaking him.

But he was unconscious, his amber eyes closed, the wide mouth unsmiling. And when she shook him, the corner of his scarf fell away and revealed the scattering of red spots across his chest.

THE DOCTOR'S face was grim as he closed his black bag and turned to Daisy.

"It's quite certain, I'm afraid," he said, beginning a lengthy washing of his hands in the basin of water he had asked for. "I've seen plenty of it lately, and you must take steps to keep the child safe, too. You may both have it already, and not know it yet. If you start to feel as though you are catching cold, you must come to me at once."

"But..." Daisy swallowed, still struggling to comprehend the dreadful word he had spoken a moment before. "*Smallpox*."

"Yes," said the doctor. "I'm terribly sorry."

He didn't look at her as he spoke, nor at Bart, who was sleeping soundly under the influence of the medicine the doctor had given him with a long glass syringe and an appallingly long and shiny needle.

Daisy clutched Fannie more tightly. The girl had fallen asleep in her arms where she sat in a chair by the stove, trembling head to foot.

"Will he live?" she asked.

"He has a good chance. He is young and strong, but he will be scarred, and he may well be blinded. Your husband is very ill, Mrs. Parker." The doctor frowned down at her. "We have immunized the child, and she will have a good chance to avoid getting very ill. You received your immunization in the workhouse. But your husband – well." He cleared his throat.

Daisy didn't know what that meant. She stared at Bart, at the swathe of sweaty hair over his forehead, the peppering of small sores around his wrist as she held his hand.

"Blinded?" she whispered, thinking of his soft eyes and the way he smiled when he looked at Fannie.

"I'm sorry, Mrs. Parker." The doctor straightened. "There is little more that I can do."

"How long will he be ill?" Daisy asked. "How – how am I to feed us in the meantime?" There were some savings tucked away in a sock behind the bed, she knew, but she didn't know if it was going to be enough.

"I can't say. Good luck," said the doctor.

He left, and Daisy sat with Bart, gently stroking his soft hair, her hand wrapped around his. How was she going to tell Fannie that she needed to stay away from her father? How was Daisy going to keep them all safe?

What was the landlord going to say, when he found out that her husband had brought smallpox to the tenement?

The landlord couldn't know, not now. For now, Daisy just had to sit here and hold Bart's hand and pray with all her heart that he would live, and not be blind, and that this wasn't the end of everything she knew and held dear.

CHAPTER 2

"MAMA." Fannie tugged at Daisy's skirt for the hundredth time that day. "Mama, I hungry."

"It's almost ready," Daisy promised, peering down into the pot on the stove. They were down to their last few shillings, and the sack of oats was dwindling quickly; as a result, the gruel was even thinner and more watery than usual.

Fannie's eyes were wide, uncomprehending, and Daisy hated the way they looked huge in her pinched face. She had no idea how it was possible that her round, happy little girl had become a bony waif in a matter of two weeks.

"I hungry," she insisted.

"Almost. Almost. Go and play with your dolly in the corner, there's a good girl," said Daisy. "You know that I want you to stay away from your papa right now."

Fannie looked over, confused, at the bed. Bart still lay stretched out there, right in the same place he'd been for the past three weeks. Daisy had been able to get him out of bed to wash and eat and use the chamber pot for the first week.

But now, her husband lay still, skeletal and wasted, his body pock-marked with pus-filled sores, his eyes deeply sunken in blackened sockets, breathing shallowly. He barely looked like a man anymore. Fannie was staring at him as though she didn't recognise her father.

A small, swift shadow crossed the room, and Fannie turned away, looking up at the window. There was a soft tap on the glass. Daisy glanced up from the gruel to look at a sparrow, perched on the windowsill, his small beak tap-tapping on the glass as though he was angry with his reflection.

"Mama, bird!" Fannie giggled, stumbling toward the window on stumpy legs, her hands held out. "Mama, catch bird."

"No, Fannie. No catching the bird," sighed Daisy, scooping out some of the gruel into a bowl. She blew on it until it seemed cool enough, then gave Daisy her small tin spoon. "Here's your dinner."

"Dinner." Fannie's eyes lit up, and she grasped the bowl carefully with both hands.

"In your corner," Daisy ordered.

Fannie gave Daisy a reproachful look, as though she'd just been scolded. Daisy didn't know how to explain that she was trying to keep Fannie safe. It just didn't seem to make sense to her, and how could it? It didn't make sense to Daisy, much less to her two-year-old. Nonetheless, Fannie toddled obediently to her corner, sank down onto the floor beside her crib, and began to gulp down her meal in huge, hungry bites.

Daisy was hungry, too, but her worry over Bart swallowed her hunger whole. She spooned some gruel into another bowl and pulled up a low stool beside her husband's bed. Her body ached with the familiarity of her perch, and she was careful not to touch any of the leaking pustules that oozed yellow fluid onto his skin. The doctor had told her to clean the pustules daily. That had been a week ago, the last time that Daisy had been able to afford the doctor.

"Bart?" Daisy tried to find somewhere to touch him that wasn't covered in the raw, oozing sores. She settled for resting a hand on his shoulder, very lightly, hoping the blankets would protect him from her touch. "Bart, darling, it's time for dinner."

Bart opened his eyes. Their softness was gone; they were cold and glassy now, like he was a long way away. But he stirred on the pillow, and his fevered eyes still found hers somehow.

"Daisy," he said. The word was more a shape of his breath than a definite sound.

"Yes, love, it's me." Daisy managed a smile. "Now here's some nice gruel for you. I put some sugar in it." She kept her voice low so that Fannie wouldn't hear; there was hardly any left, and she was keeping it for Bart.

His lip jerked and wobbled in an attempt at a smile. "It's all... right," he whispered, the rhythm of his words broken by his laboured breathing. "Not... hungry."

"Come on, darling. You have to eat. You have to keep your strength up somehow." Daisy took a spoonful of the gruel. "Just a few bites."

Bart was too weak to sit up, but he obediently opened his mouth for a spoonful of gruel and swallowed it, slowly and with great difficulty. She could see that it hurt him. That he was doing it for her.

That he was doing all of this for her. Clinging to life for her.

He sagged back onto the pillows after three or four bites, his face a mask of pain. "I'm sorry," he whispered.

"Barty, no. Don't be sorry." Daisy wrapped his hand in her own, touching the bandaged digit with tenderness. "It's all right. Have a nice rest, and then you can eat a little more, and you'll feel better soon."

It was a miracle, the doctor had said, that she and Fannie hadn't gotten ill at all. She prayed desperately that there was enough miracle left for Bart.

"Daisy, I..." Bart sucked in a long, struggling breath that rattled ominously in his throat. He looked up at her, and for a moment his eyes were warm and bright, the way they had always been, but she knew he was no better. A lance of terror ran through her.

"Hush, darling," she said, stopping him. "Just sleep now. Just sleep."

"Daisy." Bart swallowed painfully. "You must... know..."

"Don't." Daisy fought to hold back her tears. "Please, don't."

"You must." Bart raised his hand, trembling with weakness, and his cold fingertips brushed her cheek. "Don't let... this break... your heart. I... will see you... again."

Daisy was sobbing as softly as she could now, not wanting Fannie to hear.

"I can't," she breathed. "I can't."

"You will," he murmured.

"I need you. I can't be without you."

"You will... never be without... me," Bart whispered. "Look... for me... in the birds."

Daisy wiped angrily at her tears. "You're not going away," she told him. "You're going to be right here with me, and everything is going to be just fine."

His eyes were fluttering closed, and his smile was fading. "It is," he murmured. "It is. Don't... lose faith. Don't lose faith, Daisy."

She squeezed his hand. "Bart?"

He had settled back onto his pillows, his eyes closed, his breathing slow and deep. And an hour later, as twilight fell, that breathing grew slower and slower until it stopped.

❧

HOW, how was it possible that Daisy would be worrying about money at a time like this?

She trembled, clutching the little bag in her hands. It was Bart's life savings, the money he'd hoped to use to set up his shop and build their comfortable flat above it. But that dream was dead now, just as sure as Bart was, wrapped up in a shroud on the bed they'd once shared, the bed that now reeked of sickness and death. Daisy kept expecting to see him step through the door at any moment, whole and hearty and laughing to his little girl.

"*Eight* shillings?" she gasped. Bart had been lucky to make that amount of money in a full week.

"Aye, or we won't take it," said the gruff man at the door.

Daisy could only be relieved that her neighbour was looking after Fannie at this moment. She didn't want her daughter ever to hear the physical remnant of her father referred to as *it*.

"Do you want us to take the body, or don't you?" asked the other man plaintively.

"All right. All right." Daisy opened the bag and tipped the eight shillings onto her palm. Only five were left. She hid those in her bodice, quickly, as if fearful that the men would snatch them from her. Instead, they took their eight shillings and muscled past her into the house.

One of them seized Bart's shoulders, the other his feet. Daisy opened her mouth to ask them to be gentle, but what was the point?

They started to shuffle out of the room, carrying him, and one of Bart's arms unfolded from under the blanket – he had been stiff last night, in the long and dreadful hours that she had clung to him, weeping – and flopped toward the floor. His skin was putty grey, swirled with purple where it had rested against the pillow, where blood had stopped moving through his body and lay in one spot like a bruise. The hand was swollen and lumpish and misshapen with pustules.

It was then that Daisy realized that this wasn't Bart they were taking away. Bart was gone forever, and now she was completely alone.

FANNIE DIDN'T LOOK at the empty bed when Daisy's neighbour brought her back, angry and disgruntled and demanding the sixpence that Daisy had promised her for caring for the little girl for half an hour. Daisy parted with the money slowly, painfully aware that those few shillings were all they had left.

"Mama, I hungry," said Fannie, turning away from the bed and looking toward the stove.

Daisy had never been much good with numbers. How long would five shillings feed them? A week? Ten days? And then what? What would they do without Bart? How would they pay the rent on Monday? Her heart hammered painfully all over her body, as though it refused to behave and stay in her chest.

She scooped the last of the cold gruel from the pot on the stove, and Fannie went to her corner without being told to sit there. She slurped the cold gruel hungrily from her bowl.

If they couldn't pay the rent on Monday, Daisy realised with a pang of terror, then they would be evicted. She'd seen her landlord evict people before, seen how he snatched their belongings and tossed them onto the street. He was a tall, cold, brutal man who didn't care if he hurt someone, and Daisy knew that if he so much as heard the chink of coins in their little bag, he would take them.

She sat down by the kitchen table and reached for the little box on the corner where she kept her sewing things.

Counting out the coins in a neat row on the table, she lifted her hem up in front of her and laid the first one on the edge, folding it over to make a little pocket of fabric. With a few tight, careful stitches, she sewed her dress closed around the money. It was the only safe place she could think of.

With the money tucked away and her daughter fed, Daisy found her hands suddenly empty. She sat at the table, staring at nothing in an effort not to stare at the empty bed. For the past weeks while Bart was ill, Daisy had been sleeping on a blanket on the floor beside his bed, afraid that the tiniest of her stirrings in her sleep would brush against his ruined skin and prompt him to cry out in pain as he had done so many heart-wrenching times. Where would she sleep tonight? Would she crawl into that bed? She had never slept in it alone before, never. She and Bart had shared that bed on their wedding night and every night since.

The memory of that day, that glorious wedding day and the joy that followed, was more heart-wrenching than the sight of his lifeless body had been. Daisy crunched up her hands and covered her eyes with them to stop herself from crying in front of Fannie.

Fannie. The thought of being all alone with her daughter – with *Bart's* daughter – sent a wave of terror, exhaustion, and resentment through her. When she looked up at the little girl playing in the corner, Daisy suddenly wanted to run away, to leave the child. It was a repulsive instinct that she hated the moment she felt it, but the hatred only seemed to make it grow. What was she going to do next? How was she going to care for this child?

Fannie stood up and came over to her, holding out the dirty bowl. "Mama, fank-oo," she said in her little voice. It was her way of saying thank you. Daisy could remember the first time she'd said it to Bart one evening when he'd picked up her dolly from the floor and given it to her in the crib, and the memory of his delighted face shattered her. Her eyes were just as large and soft as Bart's were. *Had been.* When had the past tense become far too heavy to bear?

All at once, Daisy's grief overwhelmed her. She bent down and snatched Fannie into her arms, pressing the child close to her chest, burying her face in the thick red-gold hair, and she cried, and she cried. Fannie thrashed in her arms, uncomprehending, and began to cry too; Daisy wanted to shush her, but her grief was pouring from her like vomit, and she was powerless against it.

It was at that moment of utter heartbreak that the door to the tenement banged open with such a force that Daisy leaped back in her chair, squeezing Fannie close to her in terror. It was their landlord, filling up the entire doorway with his sheer mass.

"Mrs. Parker," he barked, heedless of the tears shining on his face.

Daisy froze in her chair, clutching Fannie tightly. It was Wednesday. She had paid the rent just two days ago. What was he doing here? She still had five nights to sleep in this tenement before their future fell apart.

"Y-yes, Mr. Munro?" she asked nervously.

Mr. Munro had small, piggy eyes that darted this way and that in his large, fleshy skull. His nose was arched and hawkish, ubiquitous on his loose-jowled face. "How dare you keep this from me," he growled, then spat, a globule of filth landing by her feet.

Daisy clung more tightly to her screaming daughter. "I – I don't understand – "

"Oh, I think you do," he roared. "Don't you know that by letting your husband rot away in his sickness here, you've exposed this entire building to that – that *plague*?"

She saw the way Mr. Munro's eyes darted around the room, as though looking for some kind of green smog to represent the miasma that contained the disease that had killed Bart. He pulled a handkerchief out of his pocket – silk, monogrammed – and held it to his mouth and nose as if to ward it off.

"Sir, they... they just took him away," Daisy whimpered. "Fannie and I are all right."

"That you may be, but you brought this plague upon this building, and you're going to get us all killed," snapped Mr. Munro. "How could you stay here, knowing what he had?"

Daisy's tears spilled over with alarming speed. "He was dying. My husband was dying," Daisy sobbed. "I was just trying to care for him, for my baby – "

"I don't want to hear it, woman," Mr. Munro thundered. He stepped back, pointing an imperious finger down the hall. "Get out!"

Daisy stared at him, her tears still rolling down her cheeks. "Wh-what?"

"I said to get out."

Daisy stumbled to her feet. "Now?"

"Yes, woman," raged Mr. Munro. "You should have left this place long ago. Now get out of my building before I call the police to drag you out."

"No. No, no, no, sir, you don't have to do that. You don't have to do that," Daisy babbled. She scrambled to her feet, setting Fannie down; the little girl screamed, reaching up to be lifted, but Daisy was stumbling over to the bed to pull off their blankets. They would need blankets.

Mr. Munro stepped into her path, his eyes almost popping out of his head. "What are you doing?"

"I – I just want to take our things, s-sir," gasped Daisy.

"Your things are contaminated with smallpox," bellowed Mr. Munro. "Do you think me a fool? Do you think I didn't know, as soon as I saw those men loading him onto their wagon?

You will take nothing from this house. It will all be burned. All of it."

Daisy's heart shattered. She thought of Fannie's crib, of the little stove where she'd cooked so many meals for them, the table where they'd laughed together so many times...

"Out!" thundered Mr. Munro. "Now!"

Daisy snatched up what few things she could – Fannie's dolly, the clean blankets from the cupboard, the single dry apple on the kitchen counter – before Mr. Munro began to wave his arms and scream at her. Then she grabbed her baby, pulled her close to her chest, and fled from the only home where she had ever been happy.

CHAPTER 3

DAISY RAN out of the building with only one thought: to get to the handcart before anyone else did.

Part of her was already burning with fear that some opportunistic soul had long since made off with the handcart, perhaps Mr. Munro himself. But it seemed his fear of smallpox was even greater than his endless greed. Mr. Munro stood in the hallway, screaming at her, while her neighbours in the building pressed themselves against the windows and ogled.

Daisy felt naked, stripped of her dignity, and tears rolled silently down her cheeks as she ran. The handcart was there, just where Bart had left it on the last happy day she would ever live, the last day of normality and chasing feathers with

Fannie and kissing a beautiful husband goodbye every morning. Now, everything was broken; Daisy felt like her life had fractured into a million razor-sharp pieces, and they cut her every time she tried to gather them up.

There was no time to worry about her pain. She had to get out of here before Mr. Munro's screams alerted the entire neighbourhood. Then no one would buy anything from her. She swung Fannie into the handcart, sitting her down amid the pots and pans, still wailing at the top of her lungs. Tossing the blanket over her and setting down the tiny box of belongings she'd been able to salvage, Daisy tugged at the handle, hauled the handcart onto the path and pushed it out onto the street.

Her heart began to slow down a little once Mr. Munro and his fierce yelling had been left behind. She knew she should sing to Fannie, to calm her, but her voice refused to carry any kind of melody, so she just shushed her until the exhausted baby curled up in the bottom of the handcart and went to sleep.

The silence cleared Daisy's head a little. She pushed the handcart into the lee of a large building and glanced around, trying to get her bearings; in her panic she had simply been walking, pushing the heavy cart, trying to escape. Now, she had found herself on the edge of a busy street lined with shops. The people moving along the pavement were well-dressed, but not so well-dressed as to think themselves above buying from a handcart peddler.

Daisy took two or three long, deep breaths. The pain in her soul was far too much to bear, even to think about; she felt as though she was carrying a mountain inside her heart. Instead, she found herself staring down at Fannie, at the one tiny piece she had left from the life she had once had. The life that now felt as though it belonged to someone else.

Something fierce and almost mechanical seemed to take charge over her mind, something that made her concentrate on simple, basic facts. They needed food. They needed shelter. They needed money. These were facts, and they were terrible, terrifying facts, but they were easier than trying to bear the mountain in her chest. She could face the facts. They were something she could defeat, unlike her grief.

Food, money, shelter. Money. It all came down to money. There were still a few things left in the handcart. Daisy could sell them. People didn't know her, but maybe they knew the cart itself, maybe they would recognise some of Bart's wares. She bent down and lifted a small box from inside the cart, then set it down in front of her. There were two knives left inside, and next to Fannie lay a pot and a pair of soup bowls.

They would be enough for a little money, perhaps enough to buy some more things, to buy food, to find a tenement. They might survive this. They had to survive this.

Fannie had to survive this. She had to keep her child alive, for the sake of... *No!* Daisy suddenly couldn't bear even to think his name. She would never say it again, she decided. She would hide it deep down inside herself, because to think about him was to pour acid on her heart.

"Knives!" she called out, holding up the box. Her voice was thin and reedy, and it railed uselessly against the cool breeze, but she had to keep trying. "Get your knives! Good, strong knives!" She hardly knew anything about knives and glanced back into the box to make sure of what kind they seemed to be. "Paring knives! Bread knives!"

People streamed past. Some glanced at her, then kept on moving. Most of them didn't spare her a second glance. Her voice was growing tired, and Fannie was beginning to stir in the cart as though she would wake, when a man stopped and looked her up and down. "Where'd you get the cart, missy?" he asked brusquely. "Used to belong to a knife peddler named – "

She couldn't let him say the name; hearing it would be unbearable. "I'm his wife," she said quickly. "His – his widow." It was the first time she had given herself that label, and it lay around her neck like an iron chain.

"Pity. He was good." The man glanced into the box. "I need a new bread knife. How much is it?"

Daisy turned over the price tag that Ba— that her late husband had attached to the knife. "That's two shillings and sixpence, sir."

"Two shillings and six!" The man barked. "Do you take me for a fool?"

Daisy stared at him. "Sir, that's the price he put on the knife. Look, it's in his hand." It was, and she forced herself not to stare longingly at the careful curve of the numbers he'd written.

The man snorted. "I'll give you a shilling and six," he said. "Not a penny more."

Daisy felt tears prickle the edges of her eyes. Why should he pay her any less than he was willing to pay Bart? What made her any different? But he seemed to be losing interest in her; he was shifting his weight, looking ready to walk away.

"All right," she said quickly. "A shilling and six it is."

The man smiled, a predatory thing, and tipped the money into her palm before snatching the knife and disappearing into the crowd.

Daisy stared down at the money in her palm for a moment before tucking it carefully into her pocket. Tonight, she would sew it into the hem of her dress with the other few coins she'd managed to hold on to. That was, if there was any money left. It would feed them for today, at least, and perhaps she could save some of it to buy more wares from Bart's supplier.

Perhaps they were going to survive this after all.

It was a symptom of how low she had sunk, Daily thought, that this alleyway felt like a Godsend.

She tried not to think too much about the piles of rubbish lying all over the alley – the broken glass and reeking scraps of rotting food, the old rags and the rat droppings scattered everywhere – and thought instead of the fact that it was tucked neatly under the overhang of an abandoned building. The building was locked up tight, but its tall brick wall and solid roof were impervious to the elements and offered shelter from the frigid rain that pattered quietly on the roof as Daisy pushed some rubbish away with her foot and stacked a few damp sticks together for a fire. She was starting to regret the fact she'd tried to save a few pennies by buying the damp wood. It smelled salty; she wondered if it was driftwood. Wondered where in the world it had washed in from. Somewhere more beautiful than this, she assumed, dragging a match across the harsh surface of the wall so that it flared golden light into the alley. The light only served to cast more of the alley's ugliness into sharp relief.

"Mama, hungry," said Fannie. She was standing up in the cart, gripping the edges with two small hands that were blue with cold. Her eyes were red; it seemed to Daisy that the child had not stopped crying for the three days since they had left the tenement behind.

"I know, love. I know." Daisy held the match to the scraps of paper she'd gathered for kindling. She prayed they would catch. They didn't; the flame sputtered and died, and Daisy's heart faltered with it. She didn't have very many matches left.

Taking a shaky breath, Daisy pulled out another match, and this time the little flame licked along the edge of the paper. She crouched down over the pathetic fire, ignoring the desperate pull of exhaustion in her arms and legs, and cupped her hands around it, blowing gently. Her fingers were burning with cold. "Come on," she whimpered. "Come on."

"Mama, hungry," said Fannie again.

"Just a little longer, love," said Daisy.

It felt like a miracle when the flame finally reached around the first of the damp sticks. Steaming and hissing, the sticks began to smoulder, and Daisy sat back, exhausted. She held out her hands to the struggling fire, but it didn't seem to make much difference.

"Mama, hungry!" Fannie's voice was gaining the edge that meant she was moments away from shrieking.

"All right. I'm coming," Daisy snapped, regretting it at once. None of this was Fannie's fault. She reached for the paper bag she'd hidden in the corner of the cart and lifted the child out with her free arm, sitting them both down on a moderately dry patch of dirt beside the fire. Fannie's little hands reached eagerly into the bag and pulled out a rough loaf of yesterday's brown bread. She tore it open and began to eat in careless, hungry gulps. It was the first food they had had all day.

There was tuppence left after buying bread and wood. Daisy would sew it into her dress tomorrow morning; now, she was too exhausted to move, almost too exhausted to lift their single blanket out of the cart and spread it on the ground beneath the handcart. Wrapping Fannie in her arms, she hugged the child close, laid her head on the cold ground, and slept at once.

Clang!

The metallic sound yanked Daisy from a sleep so deep it was almost closer to death. Her eyes snapped open. The darkness was absolute, and cold had settled over her body like a crushing weight; she couldn't feel her fingers or toes, and she realised she was shivering.

Her arms tightened convulsively around her baby, and she lay still, listening for Fannie's breathing. It was deep and regular, and the little girl's body was warm in her arms. She was all right. Daisy closed her eyes and allowed her head to slump against the ground again. If Fannie was all right, she could keep going. As long as she cared for Bart's child, there would be one way in which she had not failed him, even though his life had slipped through her fingers.

Another clang. Daisy opened her eyes, her body springing tight. The sound had come from somewhere above her. Was the wind catching one of the pots hanging on the side of the cart?

There was a soft clinking, then a rummaging sound in the cart. "There's hardly anything here," hissed a disappointed voice.

Nausea leaped in Daisy's stomach. She cringed, curling herself more tightly around Fannie, praying that the child wouldn't wake up. The voice belonged to a man, and as her eyes adjusted to the darkness, she could just make out the pair of feet inches from her face, a pale flash of skin showing through a hole in a shoe.

"We could take the cart," suggested a second voice. This one was low, and growling, and equally masculine.

Daisy clung to Fannie, trembling head to foot. They were stealing the wares. Those wares were all she had left with which to make a living. If they took them...

"Not worth much. And it'll slow us down," grunted the first.

"Fine. Give me that pot. We'll put the knives in it."

A clatter of steel on steel filled the night, making Daisy jerk with fright, and Fannie sat up suddenly, her plaintive voice ringing out through the cold air. "Mama!" she shouted.

"Shhh," Daisy cried desperately, clapping her hand over the child's mouth and drawing her into her arms again.

Frightened, Fannie screamed. There was a scrabbling sound from beside the cart, shouts of surprise; Daisy tried desperately to shush her daughter, but it was too late. A grubby hand closed around Daisy's arm, dragging her out from under the cart, ripping a scream of panic from her own lips as she clutched Fannie tightly with her free arm.

"What's this, then?" rumbled one of the men. A swinging lantern was lifted over Daisy's head, and she was squinting up into the loose-lipped face of a scruffy man with a wandering eye.

"It's a girl," said the other. "And a child. We could sell them."

"No!" Daisy shrieked, ripping her arm free of her captor's grip, and clutched her screaming child closely to her chest. "Leave me alone!"

The second man was holding the big cast-iron pot that Bart had hoped to sell for enough money to replace their tired old bedding. The sight and memory burned Daisy's eyes.

"Now there's no need for a fuss, missy," he hissed.

The first man grabbed at her again, and Daisy jumped back. "Those are my things," she shouted. She wanted to flee, but what would she do without the cart and wares?

"Grab her," growled the second man.

The first man lunged at her, and Daisy staggered back again, screaming for all she was worth, but she wasn't fast enough, and his hands closed on the back of Fannie's dress, yanking her effortlessly from Daisy's thin arms.

"Mama! Mama!" Fannie shrieked.

Daisy's world was melting around her. If that baby was taken from her, she would have nothing left, nothing. The fear in Fannie's eyes wrenched at her soul. She couldn't let anything happen to her daughter. A wordless shriek of primal rage tore from Daisy's lungs, and she flung herself at the big man holding her child, throwing herself against him so that he staggered back a step in shock. Her fingernails found his cheeks and raked down them, scrabbling toward his eyes, shrieking and shrieking in a terrible voice that she barely recognised.

"Ahh! Help! Help!" the big man yelped. "She's mad! She's mad!"

Daisy felt mad. She felt she would do anything, anything, to get her baby back, and the more the man stumbled away from her, the more she pounded her small fists against his face.

"Run!" shouted the second man.

The first man let out a final roar and let go of Fannie. Daisy heard the sickening thud as her daughter was thrown into a heap of rubbish, and spun away from the man, her arms outstretched toward her little girl. The sound of running feet filled the alleyway, and then the shrill, plaintive cry of a terrified child.

"It's all right. It's all right," Daisy gasped. She pulled Fannie into her arms, hugging her close as she hurried to the streetlamp at the mouth of the alley and held the little girl up to the light. Fannie's small face was screwed up into a scream and red with tears, her mouth wide open, tiny white teeth trembling with the force of her crying. Her dress was smeared with mud and nameless filth. But there was no blood. She was unhurt.

"My baby. My poor, poor baby," Daisy sobbed, hugging Fannie close. "It's all right. You're all right."

She staggered back to the cart and sank to the ground beside it, her back to the wall, and held the screaming baby until her crying slowed and stilled into a deep sleep born of utter exhaustion.

❧

THEY HAD GOTTEN AWAY with everything.

In the brutal dawn light, grey with clouds, Daisy stared down into the empty cart with shaking hands. The knives, the pots, even the few handkerchiefs that Bart had always kept in a corner to sell for a few pennies to the ladies – those two men had taken every piece of merchandise she had left. Even the tuppence she had hidden away in a corner. Why didn't she sew it onto her dress?

Fannie tugged at her skirt. "Mama, hungry," she said.

Daisy stared down at her. The little girl's cheeks and nose were red with cold, and her eyes were wide, pleading. Still, she seemed none the worse for wear after last night, and a flood of resolve rushed through Daisy at the sight. The men had taken everything, but they hadn't taken Fannie. As long as she had Fannie, she could keep trying.

"Let's go find something to eat, love," Daisy said. She scooped Fannie up and put her into the cart, then tugged it out of the alley and into the street. There was a puddle formed by the gutter of the abandoned building just a few feet away; Daisy crouched there and plunged her hands into the icy, murky water, washing the dried blood from underneath her fingernails.

There was nothing left to sell. The money Daisy had sewn into the hem of her dress would feed them for two or three days, but it wasn't enough to buy the kind of merchandise Bart had always sold. It would be better to find work. The thought gave her hope, and she straightened up, drying her hands on her skirt and feeling as though some of the fog of her grief was lifting. Why hadn't she tried that before? She was skilled; she could cook and sew and clean with the best of them. Surely someone would hire her as a maid.

She turned and directed her steps away from the bustling marketplaces and toward the townhouses deeper inside the city.

It was more than an hour's walk from the grubby alleyway where Daisy had slept to the beautiful, manicured homes that lined the broad street along which she was now walking. There were few pedestrians here; elegant carriages rattled by and occasional men and women on horseback casting her imperious glances. She knew she was a stain upon the face of this beautiful part of London. Her filthy, tattered dress could not have been more out of place among the tall, manicured hedges, the great sweeps of green lawn, the houses that towered up against the sky from among beautiful trees with spreading branches.

Just walking along the street was so daunting that Daisy stood in front of the servants' gate to one such townhouse for a few long, long moments, trying to pluck up the courage to enter. Fannie whined and fussed, her whimpers growing louder. A man who was trimming the lawn gave them both a severe look.

Daisy gave him a faint smile and looked down at Fannie. "Time to be very, very quiet, my sweetheart," she told the child, bending down to run a hand over Fannie's hair. It was gold and red at the same time and curled profusely around her shoulders when it was clean; now, it was just a fog of tangled blonde.

"Hungry," Fannie moaned.

Daisy's stomach clenched. She had hoped to be able to keep Fannie quiet for a little longer, but she reached into her pocket and pulled out the crust of bread she had saved last night. "Here," she said.

Fannie snatched it and began to gnaw at it as though she would devour the entire thing in seconds. Daisy would have to do this right away. She squared her shoulders, took a deep breath, and dragged the cart up the little path to the servants' door at the very back of the house.

Her hands shook as she rapped on the door. It seemed an unbearably long time before a little slip of a kitchen maid opened it and stared up at her. The girl was no older than ten, and she was tiny and skinny, but her neat little blue uniform looked blissfully whole and warm to Daisy's eyes.

"Who are you?" she asked plaintively.

"I'm looking for work," said Daisy. "Please may I speak with the housekeeper?" She pronounced each word carefully, the way Bart did, trying her best to sound more educated.

"We're lookin' for an assistant cook, I know," said the girl. She turned and disappeared into the kitchen, and Daisy waited outside, keeping half an eye on Fannie as she nibbled at the bread.

Another eternity later, an orderly woman in a well-pressed black dress that buttoned up right beneath her chin appeared in the doorway and studied Daisy for a few long moments.

"My name is Mrs. Harris," she said coolly. "I understand you're looking for work."

"Yes, ma'am," said Daisy quickly. "I can cook and clean and sew. I was a housewife for a time, and I did it all myself. But my husband is gone, Lord rest his soul, and I'm ready to do any work I can to help." She paused, breathless, staring nervously up at the housekeeper.

Mrs. Harris gave her a long look. "You've been on the streets," she observed.

"That's right, ma'am. But I have very clean and sober habits, I can promise you that. I'll work with all my heart, truly I will. I..."

"Mama!" Fannie piped up. "I drop."

Daisy whipped around. Fannie was pointing down at the half-eaten crust, which she had dropped on the path beside her. "I drop," she howled again, a scream rising in her voice.

"Is that *yours?*" Mrs. Harris asked.

Her voice was suddenly very cold. Daisy turned to look up at her, her heart hammering. "Yes, ma'am."

"And what do you propose to do with the child when you're meant to work?" Mrs. Harris snapped.

"She'll be very good," Daisy implored. "She won't – "

"I don't have time for this." Mrs. Harris turned away. "Good day."

The door crashed shut in Daisy's face.

"Mama, I drop!" shrieked Fannie.

Daisy covered her face with her hands, the morning's hope shattering. It seemed nothing could go right for her.

CHAPTER 4

DAISY'S hem felt uncomfortably light. She had grown used to the comforting weight of the coins she'd sewn into it bumping against her shins as she walked, but now, there was only one shilling left. It bounced around as she dragged the cart and Fannie back toward their old neighbourhood, her blistered hands struggling to keep their grip on the handle.

Two days. She had spent two long, long days trying to find work in the fancy houses, and it had all been useless. A few housekeepers had looked ready to hire her when she had told them what she could do; but the moment they saw Fannie, they had all chased her away.

Take the brat to a workhouse. That's the only way you'll ever find work, one of them had told her. The memory made her vision blur with tears. She blinked them back, looking over her shoulder at Fannie, who was sleeping in the cart. Her little face was already so thin and pinched. It had seemed not long ago that her cheeks had been red and rosy with health.

She could never give up Fannie. It would be giving up the last thing that was capable of giving her life any meaning.

That knowledge drove her to keep walking, despite the frigid wind that blasted down the street, ripping at her clothes and hair. That shilling would only feed them for another day or two, if they were very lucky. She wasn't going to get hired. She had to find something to sell, or all would be lost.

Turning down the next street, she tried not to remember the last time she had come here. She tried not to remember the warm, gentle pressure of Bart's hand on her own or the way Fannie had run on ahead, yelling and giggling. They had been walking home from a trip to the market when Bart had said he needed to stop by the office of the merchant who supplied him with his wares. The merchant, Mr. Dickinson, was a big, be-whiskered man who seemed to be kind enough. Maybe he would give Daisy a chance.

It was the only thing she could think of to do. She dragged the cart up to the small warehouse with the brass letters on the glass door. *Dickinson Enterprises*. There was a bell; she rung it hesitantly, then stepped back.

"Enter," barked a voice.

Daisy glanced at the sleeping Fannie. It would do her no good to bring the child inside. She let go of the cart and stepped inside, seeing instantly that this was no place where she would be considered to belong. This was a small office, a desk in the corner, a few chairs opposite; there were tall walls all around it, and Daisy imagined that this was just a walled-off corner of the warehouse.

Mr. Dickinson was sitting behind the desk, and he glared up at her, his bushy white brows touching.

"Who are you?" he barked. "There's nothing here for you to steal."

"Begging your pardon, sir, I'm Mrs. Parker," she said quickly.

"Parker? Parker?" Mr. Dickinson barked. He was rising from his chair and seemed ready to lunge across the desk and strangle her when recognition suddenly dawned in his eyes. "Wait. Parker. Mrs. *Bart* Parker?"

"That's right, sir."

"Well, where is he?" Mr. Dickinson asked impatiently. "He ordered a new set of knives and two pans, and they've been waiting here for him for more than a month."

"Yes, sir." Daisy took a long, shaky breath. "B... B..." She couldn't say his name. "My husband is gone."

"Gone? Gone where?"

"Sir, I beg your pardon, but he's dead." Saying the word was like chewing a mouthful of glass.

Mr. Dickinson sagged back into his chair, blinking at her. "How?"

"Smallpox, sir. I'm on my own now. Well, my little child and I."

"That's a pity. A real pity." Mr. Dickinson ran a hand over his magnificent white whiskers. "I'm sorry to hear that, Mrs. Parker. Bart was a good man. One of the best."

"Yes, sir." Daisy blinked rapidly, holding back her tears.

"Well, thank you for letting me know. It was high time," grumbled Mr. Dickinson. He turned his eyes back to the ledger in front of him.

"Sir, pardon me." Daisy cleared her throat. "I wanted to know if I could take that order he placed."

Mr. Dickinson looked up at her. "Did you bring the money?"

Daisy sucked in a deep breath, her hands tangling with her skirts as though she could squeeze her nervousness out of them. "I... I don't have money yet. I'll bring it to you straight away when I sell the things. I promise you, sir, I will pay you back, I – "

Mr. Dickinson shook his head. "No. I don't extend any credit."

Daisy wasn't sure what credit was, but she fully understood *no* when she heard it, as she had heard so many times over the past few days. She fought down her tears. "Sir, if you trusted my husband, you can trust me."

"I did trust your husband, but I never gave him credit either," snapped Mr. Dickinson. "No one gets credit. That's the rule."

"Sir..." Daisy began.

"Mrs. Parker, I suggest you leave my warehouse before you make me angry," he barked.

"Please, sir, I need help," Daisy sobbed. Her tears began to flow freely now. "I can't do this on my own. My little girl is going to starve. Please, sir, I have nothing. I have nowhere left to go. I can't feed my child. Sir, I can't feed my child." The sobs racked her body, ripping at her aching bones.

Mr. Dickinson rose from his seat and strode toward her, seizing her arm. Ignoring her pleas, he marched her to the door and shoved her outside again, where her sobs startled Fannie to wakefulness. The child sat up and began to whimper. Daisy turned, and Mr. Dickinson was already closing the door.

"I'm sorry, Mrs. Parker," he said again, less sharply this time. His eyes darted to Fannie. "If you can bring me the money, I'll sell you the goods. But no credit."

The door closed quietly, and Daisy sank down onto the pavement, her head in her hands. Fannie was screaming, but she had nothing left with which to console her little girl, so she let her cry.

❧

DAISY GROANED WITH EFFORT, leaning back against the handle of the cart even though her hands burned with blisters. "Come on," she moaned. "Come on."

Fannie sat in the cart, staring at Daisy with blank eyes. Her tears had washed two white trails down her filthy cheeks. The expression in that child's face tore Daisy's heart, and she gave another hard effort, but the cart's wheel was stuck on a rut in the muddy street. She fell against it, panting, her body absolutely spent.

"Mama..." Fannie began.

"Hungry, I know." Daisy leaned her head against the cart handle. She hadn't eaten for more than a day, and she'd given Fannie the last bit of potato this morning. "I'll find food for you soon, dear," she whispered through cracked lips.

It was an empty promise. She knew it, and that knowledge tore at her soul.

She pushed the cart back a foot or so and took a deep breath, then lunged against it one more time with a cry of despairing effort. This time, it bounced forward, and Daisy finally dragged it up onto the spot on the pavement among a few other handcarts. The streets were bustling; carts and people on foot hurried to and fro, and none had stopped to glance at her when she had been wrestling with the cart. People were blind to suffering, she had realised. They saw only opportunity.

Her heart faltered as she looked up and down the row of vendors on the pavement beside her. Compared with them, Daisy didn't think her cart displayed much opportunity either. She stared sadly at the few things she had packed out on her cart. A few old glass bottles she had scrounged from a rubbish heap behind a pub. Some buttons. A few pieces of string. It was all so absolutely pathetic compared to the people near her: some were selling books, others had produce or cigarettes or food.

She had rubbish.

Exhausted beyond expression, Daisy sank down onto the pavement beside her cart and hung her head between her knees, taking deep breaths. She allowed herself a moment's despair before sitting up, trying to catch the eye of passing people, although she'd long since run out of the strength to cry her wares.

A thin, plaintive voice caught her attention. "Flowers! Flowers!" it called. "Get your fresh-cut flowers! Daisies and buttercups! Lovely marigolds!"

She looked across the street to where a tiny girl, no bigger than nine or so, was standing under a lamppost. She held a few sprigs of flowers, tied with old string, in her grubby hands; but the string didn't matter. The flowers were vibrantly lovely, glowing brightly against the grey street.

As Daisy watched, a gentleman stopped and glanced over the little girl. There was a brief exchange, and coins shimmered in the girl's hands for a moment; then the gentleman rushed off with a sprig tucked into his buttonhole.

Flowers. Daisy struggled to her feet, looking off to her left. There was a park just a block away; she and Fannie had slept there under a hedge the night before, when it was raining. There had to be flowers there. She could pick them and sell them.

She gripped the cart, gritted her teeth against the pain, and stepped forward.

THERE WERE ALMOST NO FLOWERS.

Daisy stood leaning against her cart, trembling with hunger, exhaustion, and weakness, as she stared down at the single, scraggly patch of grass where a few poppies were clinging to life, their red petals faded by struggle, some of them missing. They looked nothing like the pretty flowers the girl had been selling. She could already see herself holding them up to passersby, imploring them to see her; she could already see those same passersby brushing her off as though she was no more substantial than dust.

What choice did she have? What else could she do? Daisy glanced into the cart. Fannie was sitting quietly, staring out toward the duck pond. Her quietness frightened Daisy, but right now, she was glad of it. She glanced around the pond; it was a nice day, sunny, and a few young governesses were sitting around on picnic blankets by the duck pond, watching their young charges run around. A few of the children were Fannie's age, and they were neatly dressed, with satin ribbons in their hair and little hats shielding their faces from the sun. Rosy-cheeked, plump-legged, laughing and playing.

"Play," Fannie croaked.

"No, dear. You can't play with them." Daisy sighed, turning back to the flowers. Those governesses would never let Fannie near their precious children.

She knelt down and began to carefully pick the poppies, laying them very neatly in a pile. Her hands trembled as she worked as quickly as she could, terrified to break them but also worried that some of the other peddlers surrounding the park would notice and try to take them from her. There was still some string left on the cart to tie them into small bunches, and Daisy cursed the shaking of her hands as she tried to make her bunches as quickly as she could. At least the sun was kind on her shoulders, and Fannie had gone quiet. Maybe she was asleep.

She tried not to think of her wedding bouquet as she tied another bunch of flowers. There had been poppies in it, too.

That glorious day now felt as though it had belonged to someone else. As though another person had lived that briefly happy period in her life. Surely that could never have happened to someone as miserable as she felt at this moment.

When she had tied off the last poppy and added it to her heap, a flicker of hope rose in Daisy's heart. The little bunches looked cheerful after all. Maybe someone would want them. She gathered them into her arms and turned. "Fannie, look," she said. "Mama's picked some – "

Her voice died in her throat. The cart was empty.

She tossed the flowers down on the cart and spun around, her blood rushing in her ears.

"Fannie!" she screamed, looking at once to the peddlers along the edge of the park. There was a young man among them, carefully weaving new strips of leather into the seat of a chair; her eyes rested on him for a few long seconds. Could he have taken her?

She whirled around, her eyes frantically searching the park, and then she spotted the ragged little form toddling toward one of the picnic blankets. Her relief was replaced instantly by dread as she saw that Fannie was approaching a governess as she unpacked a picnic basket for three small, well-behaved children who sat in a half-moon around her.

"No. No, no, no," Daisy gasped. She didn't know what this woman would do when she saw dirty, sickly little Fannie coming up to her children. The thought of her daughter being harmed was unbearable. She rushed toward the blanket, but it was a long way and her limbs were tired and the scene unfolded before she could stop it.

Fannie reached the picnic blanket. The governess had opened their basket, and she was lifting out little packages wrapped in brown paper, handing them one by one to her three children. As Daisy ran toward them in horror, Fannie reached for the basket.

"Fannie, no!" Daisy cried.

It was too late. Fannie lifted one of the packages out and ripped off the brown paper to reveal a cucumber sandwich. Immediately, she raised the sandwich to her mouth and took a massive bite, chewing open-mouthed. The governess turned to reach into the basket, noticed the missing package, and looked up at Fannie.

Daisy's heart crashed to a halt in her chest.

"Well, hello," said the governess, her calm voice floating across the still air toward Daisy. "What's your name?"

Daisy stumbled to a halt, shocked. The governess seemed utterly calm. She smiled at Fannie, who was still chewing her mouthful. Fannie considered her for a moment before speaking.

"Fannie."

"Well, it's nice to meet you, Fannie," said the governess. She had very soft brown eyes, and they glanced over Fannie's ragged little dress and bony limbs. "Would you like an apple?" she asked softly.

Wide-eyed, Fannie nodded, and the governess reached into her basket and produced a juicy red apple, which Fannie snatched and held close to her chest in one hand while she held the sandwich in the other.

Daisy knew that their luck would run out at any moment; people always had a limit to their kindness. She ran up to Fannie's side and grabbed the little girl's arm, feeling with agony how thin it had become.

"I'm so sorry, miss," she burst out. "I just took my eyes off her for a minute."

The governess smiled up to her. She had thick auburn locks framing her gentle eyes, and they quietly took in the state of Daisy's clothes and the way her hand shook on Fannie's arm.

"That's all right," she said, with an easy laugh. "Cookie always packs far too much food for our little outings, doesn't she, children?"

The three clean, well-behaved children nodded.

"Would you like a sandwich?" asked the governess, incredibly reaching into the basket and producing another package.

Daisy stared from the girl to the package, and a sudden sense of shame washed through her. Why was it so much harder to take something from a sweet, generous young woman like this? She wanted to refuse, but her body screamed for nourishment, and she reached out and took the sandwich.

"Thank you," she said, trembling at the weight of the package in her hands. It made her instantly forget her manners, and she tore it open and began to devour it with the same speed as Fannie did. It was gone in moments, and Daisy was a little breathless, but it felt wonderful to have something in her stomach.

The girl smiled, sorrow in her eyes. "God be with you," she said, quietly and sincerely.

Daisy wasn't sure God was anywhere near at that moment, but if He was, He was shining in the eyes of that young governess. But the basket was empty now. Daisy felt guilty even for glancing into it to check. She gripped Fannie's arm and led the child away, tucking her back into the handcart. Now that she had eaten something, Daisy was beginning to feel that maybe those poppies would sell after all.

She dragged the handcart out of the park and started heading down the street past the peddlers, finding an empty space behind the young man with the chair. He glanced up as she pulled the handcart in beside him. "Hello," he said cheerfully.

Daisy gave him a nervous look. No one ever greeted her, but there didn't seem to be anything other than calm friendliness in his eyes.

"Afternoon," she mumbled, arranging her poppies on the front of the cart. Fannie had already devoured the apple, core and all; she curled up in the bottom of the cart and was asleep in seconds.

Daisy leaned on her cart and watched people pass by. It was a Saturday, and people were moving more slowly, their eyes resting on each cart as they walked by the peddlers. A few stopped to look at the bits of furniture the young man was selling. They looked as though he'd rescued them from the rubbish and repaired them; he sold a few small things, and Daisy began to grow used to his calm, deep voice beside her.

It was the second good thing about the entire afternoon. It wasn't long before clouds began to gather, and the sun disappeared, a chilly wind rushing down the street. Daisy pulled the blanket over Fannie, who was still asleep, and envied the child's blissful unconsciousness. No one had even stopped to look at her poppies, and they were wilting before her eyes.

When it began to rain, Daisy knew that her efforts had failed, as they usually did. She tried to hold back tears as she carefully picked up the floppy, wilted bundles of flowers, setting them inside the cart, hoping that maybe she could press or dry them somehow and sell them later. Fat raindrops splashed against her face, hiding her tears. It was time to give up and find somewhere to sleep.

She wiped at her tears and gripped the handcart, and a soft voice spoke beside her.

"Ma'am? Excuse me?"

Daisy looked up. It was the young man whose cart was beside hers. He had no hat, and his hair was slicked down to his face with rain. She realised with a jolt that his eyes were the palest grey, piercing against his dark hair.

"Wh-what is it?" Daisy stammered, shrinking back from him.

"Here, ma'am." The young man held out a hand, and Daisy jumped, then realised that he wasn't reaching out to grab her. He was offering her something, a paper bag on his palm. She took it nervously, opening the bag a little to peer inside. The round shapes of two brown, speckled eggs lay in the bottom.

"They're hardboiled," said the young man.

Daisy looked up at him, tears stinging the backs of her eyes. "I... I don't have any money."

"It's all right. I don't need the eggs," said the young man.

Daisy stared at him for a moment. His piercing eyes glanced away, as though embarrassed by the attention.

"The name's Jack," he offered after a second. "Jack Honor."

"It's nice to meet you, Jack," said Daisy, startled by the words. She couldn't remember when last she'd exchanged simple pleasantries with another person on the streets. "I'm Daisy Parker."

"Nice to meet you, too," said Jack. "You're a flower-seller?"

Daisy laughed, the sound harsh and bitter. "I sell anything I can," she sighed. "I'm a widow." The word had become just a fact now, just another hard reality of her desperate scrabble for existence.

"I'm sorry to hear that, ma'am," said Jack.

She studied him, her curiosity rising. It was strange to talk with someone, apart from Fannie, who wasn't trying to hurt or exploit her, and somehow, she didn't want the conversation to end. "Do you know where I can find flowers? I tried selling these poppies, but they're just wilting."

"I think the flower girls get them from Covent Garden," said Jack. "Or another root-seller, or some such."

"I need wildflowers," said Daisy.

He looked crestfallen. "I'm sorry. I haven't seen wildflowers in ages, besides them poppies."

The rain pelted down on Daisy's head. She raised her hands to shield her eyes from it, and Jack backed away. "You'd best be going somewhere off to shelter, ma'am," he said, "but tell you what – come back here when you're ready to sell somethin'.

Some people can be awful to peddlers. But you'll be safer here."

Daisy searched his eyes. So many men had tried to proposition her over the past miserable weeks that suspicion was her natural first instinct. But Jack's eyes were soft, and there was nothing dangerous in them.

"Thank you, Jack," she said softly. "I'll do that."

He touched his forelock and smiled brilliantly. "See you, then."

Daisy tugged the handcart forward, and immediately one of the wheels caught on a stone. She yanked on it, hard, and it lifted and moved effortlessly after her. When she looked back, Jack had a hand on the back of the cart, helping it over the bump.

THE RAIN CONTINUED ALL NIGHT. Twice, the spot Daisy had chosen to park the handcart flooded; twice she crawled out from underneath it, waking Fannie, and dragged it somewhere else. The third time, when she'd tucked the cart into a lee behind a bakery, and when it had taken her hours to get the screaming Fannie to fall asleep again, and the rain still found them and slowly began to soak through their blanket, Daisy gave up. She pillowed Fannie's head on her arm and tried her best to keep the baby out of the growing puddle around them but resigned herself to the dampness seeping into her own clothes.

As shivers took hold of her body and plucked mercilessly at her exhausted muscles, Daisy closed her eyes and buried her face in Fannie's unwashed hair. What was she going to do? They had the eggs that Jack had given them, but Daisy had seen his thin, bony hands, the few pennies he made selling bits of repaired furniture. Jack had nothing. She couldn't count on his kindness, or on the kindness of a random, sweet governess. They had helped her, and that was all that had kept her and Fannie alive today.

She couldn't gamble her entire life on kindness. How was she going to feed Fannie tomorrow? The two eggs would have to be enough for the whole day. And after that? What then? How was she going to feed her baby?

How was she going to keep one last piece of Bart alive?

The rain droned. The water soaked Daisy's clothes. Her despair felt the same; something cold and heavy, seeping to her skin and dragging her down. Out of sheer exhaustion, she slept at last.

"Mama, bird!"

Daisy ignored Fannie's cry, gritting her teeth as she gripped the ragged old shirt in both hands and pulled. She could hear threads popping, but the shirt refused to tear. Panting, she relaxed back against the cart, where she was sitting in the watery sunshine and trying to tear this shirt into even pieces. It could hardly be called a shirt at all anymore; some of the holes in the back and front were larger than the armholes, but if Daisy could tear it into rags, perhaps someone would buy them for a few pennies.

She'd already given Fannie both of the eggs. Her own belly cramped hollowly, and she knew it wouldn't be long before the girl was hungry again. And then what would she say to her? How would she explain that there just wasn't any food? How long would it be before Daisy could touch a morsel herself again?

She pushed the thoughts aside and gripped the shirt again, pulling with all of her strength.

"Mama, bird!" Fannie said again, pointing.

"Not now, dear," growled Daisy through gritted teeth. Finally, a ripping sound, and the shirt yielded in her hands. A palm-sized chunk ripped off in Daisy's hand. She stared at it, dismay flooding her. This was useless. She might as well try to sell the whole thing.

"Bird," Fannie shrieked. "Mama, catch bird!"

"Fannie," Daisy scolded, her despair and fear and hunger spilling out as irritation. "I'm not going to catch the bird."

"Mama, bird," Fannie shouted.

Daisy groaned and set the ragged shirt down on the cart. She looked up. They had stopped at the bottom corner of the park, against the river; the peddlers were all on the other side of it. She had longed to join them and take up her spot beside Jack, if it was still open, but it was pointless unless she had something to sell.

A tree was towering over them, its green buds lending colour to the day, and Fannie was pointing up into it. "Bird," she said.

Daisy sighed, looking up at the little yellow weaver that was hopping from twig to twig. "Yes, Fannie. Bird." She sighed.

She watched as the weaver hopped over to a nest dangling from a nearby twig. A female weaver, brown and green, appeared and started hopping around it.

Tears filled her eyes. She and Bart had been newly married when they'd sat on a bench watching a female weaver inspecting the nest the male had built for her. It hadn't satisfied the little bird, and she'd destroyed it, sending the nest plummeting to the ground.

Daisy could still hear Bart's chuckle. *I promise you, the house I'll build for you someday will be as perfect as you are*. She had laughed. She'd told him that any house with him in it was perfect enough for her, and it was true.

"Bird," said Fannie. "Bird house." She was pointing at a different nest now; shabby, grey, and abandoned.

"Nest," said Daisy.

"Nest," Fannie echoed.

Daisy stared at the nest, then down at the ragged shirt on her cart. Would someone buy a weaver's nest, for kindling perhaps? She couldn't stomach the thought of breaking down the nest that the female weaver was climbing around in, but the disused one would do better for kindling. At worst, they could use it themselves to light a fire that night.

"Stay here, Fannie," she ordered. The tree wasn't very tall and had a deep fork in the bottom. Daisy gripped its branches and hauled herself up into the fork, clambering toward the nest. Branches whipped across her face; she bit her lip against the pain and climbed a little higher. Stretching out her right hand, she reached for the nest. Almost there. She just needed to stretch a tiny bit more...

Her left hand slipped hideously on the tree. She yelped, lunging despairingly for the nest. It crackled in her fingers, and her left hand caught on a knot in the bark, searing pain ripping across her palm, but she didn't fall. She clung to the branch and scrambled back down, the nest clutched in her hand.

"Mama bird nest," squealed Fannie.

Daisy bit back tears of pain as she opened her left hand. There was a smear of blood across her palm. She clenched her fist, taking deep breaths, and set the nest down beside the rags. It was a sad, crumpled little thing to be selling, but if she could get only a penny, then maybe... what? It wasn't enough to buy a single loaf of bread.

There was a soft thud, and Daisy looked up to see a fresh nest lying on the paving in front of her. When she looked up, the female weaver was gone, and the male was sitting dejectedly on a twig, staring down at his nest where it lay on the ground.

"Sorry, little bird," Daisy whispered, grabbing the nest, and placing it on the cart beside the first one. She looked up at him. "She doesn't know what she had."

She grasped the cart, flinching at the pain in her bleeding hand, and pulled.

PART II

CHAPTER 5

One Year Later

Mrs. Gordon's mouth became a puckered hole when she was angry, and she was almost always angry, especially at this moment. She had no teeth left, and the rest of her face seemed perilously close to falling into the black hole of her mouth, as though the sheer vitriol of her words was sucking at her features like gravity.

"This can't go on," she declared. "I can't stand the sight of you anymore."

Daisy's heart sank. She had been waiting for this moment for weeks, and had known it was coming, yet it was still a dreadful shock. When she'd offered to buy firewood for the winter in exchange for a place to sleep in Mrs. Gordon's horrific little tenement, she'd secretly hoped the old woman would grow used to sharing the cost and keep them on year-round. The past few weeks, however, Mrs. Gordon had started growing more and more irritable.

"I'm so sorry, Mrs. Gordon," she stammered out, grabbing for a rag, and wiping at the milk that Fannie had just spilled on the old wooden box that they used as a table. The room was cramped and tiny; there was barely space to walk between the miserable little fireplace, the makeshift table, and the two pallets where they slept.

"Sorry, Mama," said Fannie.

"It's all right, dear." Daisy managed a smile.

"It is *not* all right," shrieked Mrs. Gordon. "That child is a danger. It's wasting money that we don't have." Her cries rose to a scream, and she jabbed an angry finger at Fannie, whose little face crumpled, and she began to cry.

"Shhh, shhh. Don't cry, darling." Daisy scooped Fannie into her arms.

"I'll give you something to cry about," snapped Mrs. Gordon, reaching over and giving Fannie's calf a hard pinch.

The child howled.

"Mrs. Gordon, please," Daisy cried.

"Oh, now you're going to talk back to me?" shrieked Mrs. Gordon. She threw up her gnarled, gritty hands. "That's it. That's the last straw. Out! Out! Out!"

Daisy's heart trembled within her. She and Fannie had stayed with Mrs. Gordon for three months; they had agreed the arrangement would only be until the spring, but she could hear the cold rain outside, and the thought of having to sleep out there again was horrific. "Mrs. Gordon..." she began.

The old woman's crazed, yellowing eyes rolled in her head. "Out! Out! Out!"

Fannie's screams reached a wild pitch.

"All right. All right." Daisy felt hopeless resignation flood her heart. She put Fannie down on the floor and hurried over to her sleeping pallet, where she'd rolled up their few belongings in their blanket, fearing this day would come. "We're going."

Mrs. Gordon went on shrieking, and Fannie went on crying, even when Daisy had gathered up the blanket in her arms and the child onto her hip and stumbled out of the cellar tenement and into the filthy street. It was still raining, and everything smelled of mud. Daisy lifted Fannie into the cart, tucking their blanket in beside her, and gripped its handles to tug it out of the deep mud by the front of the tenement. Mrs. Gordon's shrieks pursued them down the street.

"Why she so angwy, Mama?" Fannie asked.

Daisy sighed. "Because she's old and alone and in pain, darling."

She wanted to be angry, too. Because although she wasn't old, and although Fannie was with her, Daisy, too, lived in a world of pain.

❧

THE MORNING'S scavenging around the rubble heaps in their area had been more productive than usual. Daisy had managed to come up with several bottles that weren't even cracked, as well as a few shoelaces pulled off rotten shoes that had been thrown out behind a hotel. Rooting through the rubbish behind a nearby brothel had also yielded a torn jacket, which had had half a packet of cigarettes in the pocket. Daisy thought they were filthy things, but people would buy them, and so she would sell them.

It was not yet noon when she pushed her cart over to the spot beside the park where she had been selling her wares for a year now, and the rain had stopped, but the day was still damp and grey and cold. The day only seemed to get greyer and colder when they reached their usual spot and the place beside them was conspicuously empty.

Daisy tried to ignore the pain that seized her heart at the sight of Jack's empty place. He'd been so lovely to them for the months that she had parked her cart beside his every single day. There were times when they were able to share scraps of food; even when they both had nothing, Jack never seemed to lose the spark in his heart. He would always play and joke with Fannie, teasing laughter out of the little child even on the worst days. Daisy wished he was here now.

Fannie was standing up, gripping the edges of the cart. "Where Jack?" she asked, disappointment already hovering in her voice.

"I told you, darling," said Daisy. "We won't be seeing him anymore."

"Why?" Fannie stared up at her, eyes limpid and sad. "Where Jack go?"

"He had to move, don't you remember? Because of that man." Daisy sighed, nodding her head across the street, toward the used furniture store. There were chairs and tables on display inside, all of them just as cheap as the bits of furniture that Jack had always patched up and sold in the spot right here beside Daisy. Her heart stung at the memory, and she felt her eyes burning.

She could so easily remember the day at the beginning of winter when Jack had told her he had to move. Those beautiful eyes of his were filled with agony. *I'm sorry, Daisy. I don't have a choice. I need to find somewhere else, somewhere that people will still buy my wares, or I'll starve.*

She squeezed her eyes shut in a bid to hold back her tears. Taking shaky breaths, she arranged their few items on the cart for sale and tried to look cheerful for the sake of her guests.

"Miss Jack," said Fannie in a tiny voice.

"Me too, darling," sighed Daisy. "Me too."

She missed everything about him: his sweet voice, his smile, and most especially the way he could make Fannie smile even on the most dismal of days. She missed feeling that there was someone in the world who cared for her and Fannie. Someone to whom they both mattered.

He'd tried to persuade them to come with him, worried about the street thugs who'd been steering clear of Daisy because they often saw her with Jack. But that was right after they managed to scrounge their way into the tenement with Mrs. Gordon. Daisy couldn't face the possibility of a winter on the streets, not even for the sake of staying near Jack, and she knew that he slept beneath his cart just like she and Fannie had done.

Just like they would have to do again now.

Daisy gripped one of the bottles and held it up bravely. "Glass bottles! Get your glass bottles!" she called feebly. "Only a penny each!"

Her voice was swiftly drowned out as the other peddlers cried their wares, wares that seemed far more worth buying: food and clothes, matches and firewood. Daisy's heart shuddered within her. It looked as though this would be another hungry day for her.

So many of her days were hungry, and the hunger went far deeper now that Jack was gone. The hunger of her stomach was something she'd grown used to. But she wasn't sure she could ever learn to live with her starving heart.

JACK'S CHEST burned ominously as he hammered another slat onto the chair, scowling in dissatisfaction at the rough wood. It was the best he could get – stripped from a discarded pallet, and hardly any better than firewood – but the surface was rough no matter how hard he tried to sand it down. And sandpaper was so expensive that he dared not risk too much on a single bit of wood to fix a chair that might never sell.

Three chairs were packed out beside him where he sat at the back corner of a marketplace, the only spot he could find where no one drove him off for his scruffy appearance. He hadn't sold anything in days. Trying to ignore the hunger that sucked at his insides, Jack gritted his teeth and hammered in another nail, his hands shaking with weakness and cold.

It was at moments like these that his mind, casting about for comfort like a weary fisherman in an empty ocean, so easily took him back to last summer. Perhaps that had been the only time he had ever truly been happy. It had been a better time – warmer, and people had bought his chairs, and sometimes he had even had a little food to share. But his joy in that time truly lay in one person: Daisy Parker.

The sound of her name in his mind was enough to bring a smile to his lips and tears to his eyes at the same moment. He selected a new nail, balanced it carefully on the edge of the slat, and started to hammer it down in shaky movements. Daisy had been able to brighten his world simply by her existence. Her cascade of dark hair, tied back neatly in a stern little bun every morning, and her glorious blue eyes had been the first of her attributes to catch his eye. But it was far more than her beauty that had captured him. It was the ferocity within her, the way she held Fannie, the way she looked at the world as though she would fight armies and move mountains for her daughter. Jack had never seen someone love like that before. It made him long to be loved in that way. It made him long to feel the power of that love burning within his own heart.

The only thing burning in his chest now, though, was his lungs. He had to pause, covering his face with an elbow, and allow the terrible, racking cough to shudder through his body, feeling as though it was strong enough to rip bone and sinew apart. Breathless with coughing, Jack rested his arm on the half-finished chair and leaned his forehead against it, panting.

Was Daisy safe without him? She had told him she would be, that people among the peddlers knew her now and wouldn't allow harm to come to her. But Jack wasn't sure. He'd grown up on these rough streets; he knew how fickle people could be if they thought that they could take something from one. He imagined Daisy in a cozy little home, with plenty of food, with books and toys for Fannie, with shelter from the elements. His heart ached bitterly within him. All he wanted was to be able to do something like that for her.

But he couldn't even feed himself.

He sat back against the chair, chest heaving, his arms too tired to go on. The market square was bustling, but no one spared him a second glance. With a dreadful certainty, Jack realised that he wasn't going to be able to sell any of these chairs today.

He rose to his feet slowly and painfully, then began to stack the chairs back into his handcart, moving like an old, old man. If he couldn't sell anything here, there was no point in staying here. The fever burning over his skin made him wonder if there was any point in anything anymore.

If this fever was going to kill him, there was one thing that he wanted to do before he died. He wanted to see Daisy Parker one last time.

FANNIE STOOD on tiptoe in the cart, stretching her arm over the side. "Mama, bottle," she shouted.

Daisy, who was poking through the other side of the rubbish heap behind a row of shops a few blocks away from the park, looked up from the nondescript filth at her feet. Fannie stretched even further. "Bottle, there," she cried.

Moving over to her, Daisy just spotted the glint of glass under a heap of dirty rags. Nudging them aside with her foot, she bent down and pulled out a dark blue medicine bottle. It was empty, its cork gone, but there wasn't a crack or a chip in the glass.

"Well done, Fannie." Daisy summoned a smile, turning to the little girl. "You found it."

Fannie beamed, her grey eyes lighting up brilliantly. So much like Jack's eyes, Daisy thought, and the pang of longing that ran through her was as painful as a cramp. She handed the bottle to Fannie, who set it down carefully in the bottom of the cart, all on its own.

Distantly, a church bell tolled. Daisy counted the strokes. Twelve noon. Her heart quailed within her. It was now two days since Daisy had last eaten, and approaching twenty-four hours since Fannie's last meal, and their entire morning's scavenging had yielded only this one bottle. She was faced now with a decision that seemed to have no right answers: return to the park and use what daylight was left in the afternoon to peddle this single bottle, yielding perhaps only a penny or two, or keep scavenging and risk not having the time to sell whatever she found, guaranteeing that she and Fannie would go hungry?

"Mama, I hungry," said Fannie softly.

"I know, darling. I know." Daisy gripped the cart and tugged it forward, heading along the back of the row of shops, stopping by the nearest rubbish bin. She lifted the lid, and a cloud of flies and foul stench rose into the air, making her gag. Sometimes she could scrounge an apple core or a crust for them from the rubbish, but this was all mouldy and filthy, and when she peered into the bin, maggots writhed in the bottom.

Her stomach lurching, Daisy replaced the lid and pulled the cart onward, opening the next bin. This one was freshly emptied; there were only a few grubby scraps of damp paper and a tangle of human hair in the bottom.

Rooting through rubbish to feed her daughter. The agony and shame of it all was not as fresh as it had been right after Bart's death, but it seemed to have grown in sheer weightiness, and pressed down on Daisy's chest now as though it would crush the very breath from her.

She closed her eyes and prayed because no one else was left to listen to her. *Oh, God, help me.* A pitiful prayer, but what else did she have to give?

"Mama, bird," said Fannie suddenly. "There."

Daisy looked up, following the child's pointing finger, but all she saw was this disused alley and the rubbish bins and the greyness of the sky above.

"No, darling. There's no bird here," Daisy sighed. If she was a bird, she would never come here. She would spread her wings and fly somewhere more beautiful, somewhere where food was abundant and the sunshine felt warmer.

"Bird," said Fannie again. "Look, Mama." She was pointing at the third rubbish bin, just ahead of them. "In there, bird."

Daisy tugged the cart closer; she wanted to investigate this rubbish bin for food or something she could sell in any case. A faint, golden glint caught her eye, and she gasped. Fannie was right – there *was* a bird: not a real one, with flesh and feathers, but stamped into the spine of what looked like...

"A book!" Daisy gasped, flinging the lid of the rubbish bin aside. This was a wonderful find. She lifted the book from the bin, wiping filth from its cover; it was banged up and dirty, but there didn't seem to be any pages missing.

"Bird," breathed Fannie, her eyes alight.

Daisy couldn't read much, but when she flipped through the pages, she saw that there were pictures. She held out the book to Fannie, who took it, gasping at the golden bird on the spine. And there were more books, too. They lay in the bin, missing covers and spine, some of them with torn and crumpled pages, but Daisy knew she could sell them, and she could get real money for them, too. Perhaps a whole shilling each. That would feed them for days, even allow her to buy firewood.

"Yes. Yes," she breathed, feeling saved. She hugged the books to her chest, feeling tears sting her eyes. "Thank God. Thank God."

Maybe He was listening after all.

CHAPTER 6

Daisy hastened back to her spot by the park and set out the books as neatly as she could on her cart, using one of yesterday's rags dampened in a puddle to wipe them as clean as she could. There were six of them, an untold treasure by Daisy's standards, even though Fannie screamed when she pried the bird book from the girl's small hands.

"Book," Fannie shrieked, clinging to it.

Daisy wrested it from her daughter's hands, hushing her as she glanced up and down the street. She didn't want Fannie's tantrum to drive people away. "I'll buy you a whole apple," she promised the child. "A whole apple all for yourself, when we sell this book."

Fannie gave a last, longing look at the golden bird, but her hunger trumped all. She sat quietly in the cart as Daisy stood beside it, her heart racing, waiting for someone to notice the books.

It was only minutes later that a young woman, shabbily dressed and with haunted eyes, came to a halt beside the cart. "Oh! Look," she said to her young companion, reaching for the bird book. "It's that old story about the sparrows. Do you remember Papa reading this to us, in better times?"

"I do." The young girl smiled, her eyes misty with tears.

"I wonder what happened to that copy." The woman ran a hand over the cover, then looked up at Daisy. "How much is it?"

"One shilling, miss," said Daisy.

"Well, I suppose I *am* a parlour-maid now," said the woman. She handed over the money, and Daisy all but snatched it from her hand. A whole shilling!

The women walked away, and Fannie looked up at Daisy with shining eyes. "Do I get an apple?" she breathed.

"Yes, darling," said Daisy. "Apple."

DAISY STOOD WATCHING the old cobbler through the window for a long time, struggling to pluck up her courage. It was so difficult to find courage in herself when she felt so utterly empty: empty of heat, of love, of food, of hope, of rest. Her bones ached; her stomach felt hollowed-out, shrivelled, forgotten. It had been more than a week since she'd found those books in the rubbish, and while the first four books had yielded a shilling each and for a time, she and Fannie had eaten every night, these last two seemed incapable of being sold.

She looked down at the two books cradled in her arms. One was completely missing its cover and spine. The other had both, but they were both peeling away from the pages, making them almost impossible to turn. She couldn't count the number of times people had come up to the cart in the past two days to lift the books, glance over their titles, exclaim over the writing, until both she and Fannie began to hope that they might be able to get something to eat for the first time in days. Then they would shake their heads over the poor condition of the books and lay them down on the cart again, walking away and taking their hope with them.

Daisy had one sixpence left. She had sewn it into her dress for desperate times, and she knew that times were desperate now. Fannie had grown pale and quiet with hunger. She needed food, and people were saying that a late snow was coming. They needed firewood, too. Daisy *had* to sell these books.

She had no choice but to push the door open and step into the cobblers' shop, clutching the books in front of her as though for protection.

"H-hello?" she stammered.

The cobbler was bent over a pair of shoes at his workbench. He looked up at her over half-moon glasses, a deep frown crossing his face as he took in her ragged dress, the same dress with which she'd fled her tenement after Bart died. His expression soured instantly. It was a look that Daisy knew well; a look that saw her as an irritation instead of a human being whose life was falling apart. Had fallen apart, in honesty, long ago.

"What do you want?" he growled. "I don't give money to beggars."

"If you please, sir, I'm not a beggar," Daisy stammered out. "I just want to buy some glue."

The cobbler's glare deepened. "I'm a cobbler. Not a glue-seller."

"I know that, sir, but please, I didn't want to leave my little girl." Daisy gestured across the street to the carts lining the park. "I sell things right across the street..."

The cobbler huffed, already tired of her, and shoved a small pot in her direction. "Here."

"Oh, thank you, sir!" Daisy hurried over and lifted the pot, peering inside. There was only a little glue left in the bottom, but it would be enough.

"That'll be eightpence," the cobber snapped.

Daisy's heart faltered. She looked down at the glue, then down at the sixpence she'd sewn into her hem, then up at the cobbler. His expression told her that protest would be futile, but she had to try.

"Please, sir, I only have sixpence," she whispered. "It's all I have. Please, I... I'm hungry, and my little girl..."

The cobbler snatched the glue from her hands. "Get out of my shop," he barked. "Now. Now!"

A sob tore itself from Daisy's throat before she could stop it, and she turned and staggered out of the shop, tears rushing freely down her cheeks. What had she done to deserve the world's ire? She was desperate, so desperate, and now she would spend her last sixpence on food, and then what? They might eat tonight, but what of tomorrow? Her heart was a turmoil of despair, and more than anything, she was tired. She was so, so tired of the constant struggle to eke out an existence in this hateful world, to cling to a life that seemed to be doing its best to shake her off.

Perhaps she would have lain down in the snow and allowed the winter to take her a long time ago—if it had been about her. But it wasn't. It was about Fannie, the last piece of Bart Parker left in the world, and she had to keep fighting, she had to, she had to.

Drying her eyes on her sleeve, Daisy looked toward her cart, and her heart stuttered in her chest. A man was standing by it with his back to her. He looked thin and bedraggled, and she could hear him coughing from where she stood; a wet, diseased sound. Fannie was looking up at him, laughing and smiling.

She had no idea what men would do to a little girl like her. Daisy abruptly remembered the thugs who had tried to tear Fannie from her arms last year.

She strode across the street, raising her voice. "Fannie!" she shouted. "Look out! Don't – "

The man turned around, and Daisy froze, rooted to the spot, her words stuck in her chest.

It *was Jack.*

She hadn't seen him in three months, but those beautiful eyes of his brought back a rush of emotion stronger than anything she had felt in what seemed like forever, and she realised with a terrible pang that she loved him. The realisation made her hands shake. She stumbled forward on legs that felt numb and useless, her words coming breathily. "J-Jack, is that you?"

He smiled, and something surged within her. She wasn't sure that it was welcome, not so soon after Bart, but she was as powerless against it as a feather in the wind.

"Daisy, it's good to see you," he said, his voice thin and shaky. She saw, then, the black circles around his eyes, the sallow pallor of his cheeks, the way that his ragged clothes hung on his frame as though they'd been draped around a skeleton.

"Jack! Jack!" Fannie giggled, clapping her hands together, her pain and hunger forgotten. In the child's bright eyes, Daisy saw a shadow of the daughter she'd had before Bart's death, just as she always did when Jack made her smile.

"I'm so glad you're here," Daisy managed. She wanted to throw her arms around him, but it would be improper, so she just hugged her books more closely to her chest. "Are you moving back?"

He looked away. "I'm afraid not," he said softly. "I just..." He stopped, coughed, a raw and meaty sound. "I just happened to be nearby, and had to stop by and see you two," he croaked.

Jack was sick. Daisy pushed down her terror and smiled; it came naturally for the first time in months. "I wish I had something to share with you."

"I don't need anything. Just to see you two." Jack smiled. "Fannie tells me you're selling books now."

"Trying to." Daisy sighed, laying the two beaten-up books down on the cart. "I'm trying to get some glue to repair these, but I'm not having any luck."

Jack frowned, reaching for the books, and turned them this way and that. "It won't be hard to mend these. I have some glue back in my cart. I could glue them for you."

Gratitude flooded through Daisy's heart. She'd almost forgotten how wonderful it was to have an ally in the world, someone who would stand beside her.

"Oh, Jack, that would be wonderful," she said eagerly. "I'll share the money with you."

He shook his head, giving her another faint smile. "It's all right. I want to help you." He reached out and took the books, giving Fannie a last tickle on the cheek. "Be good, little bird," he told her. "I'll be back tomorrow morning."

"Thank you. Thank you so much," Daisy breathed.

"Bye-bye, Jack," said Fannie, waving.

"You will be back, won't you? Tomorrow?" Daisy asked, needing reassurance. Needing something to hold onto.

"I'll be back," he told her. And he smiled.

He turned and walked away, his movements slow and stiff, and Daisy wondered where his cart was. Why hadn't he brought it along with him? There was something strange about the way he was moving, but she was full of relief that someone was trying to help her, and that it was Jack.

And that they could spend that last sixpence on bread.

❧

THE BREAD WAS rough and stale, but to Daisy's starved mouth, it was the most delicious food ever made. She and Fannie sat huddled around a small fire made from a bit of driftwood she'd fished out of the river, which rushed past them just a few feet from the tiny fire that sputtered and smelled salty and spat wisps of black smoke into the air. It was cold down here by the river, but at least the bridge over their heads provided some protection from the spring drizzle that had been coming down all afternoon.

Daisy took another bite of the bread, stretching out her aching feet to the fire, its feeble heat thawing her toes. She felt warmer than she had in months, and not just because of the fire.

It was because of Jack.

With one arm draped around Fannie and their backs to the cart, Daisy leaned her head back, chewing her mouthful of bread, and closed her eyes. The world was a better, kinder, more beautiful place for Jack's presence, and she thought of the realisation that had rushed through her like a wave earlier that day. How had she fallen in love so insidiously? And so soon after Bart...

She stared up at the rough stone of the bridge above her, remembering his last words to her. *Don't lose faith, Daisy*. The memory made her heart feel squeezed, and she thought of her prayer last week, right before she'd found the books. Right before Jack had returned. If Jack was God's gift to her, then she wasn't going to spurn him. Faith was all she had left.

They finished the bread, and Fannie curled herself up tightly beside Daisy, falling asleep in moments. With her feet warmed by the fire, Daisy closed her eyes, sleep coming for her swiftly...

A jolt knocked the sleep from her mind in an instant. Daisy sat up, her arms tightening convulsively around Fannie. The fire was still burning, and Daisy heard the rumble of wheels.

Handcart wheels.

She flew to her feet, spinning around as two boys hauled at the cart, pulling it away from her up the riverbank.

"Hey!" she roared. "Stop!"

The two boys looked up at her, one pulling, one pushing. The pushing one straightened, and with a nasty shock Daisy realised that he was tall, with a mean, scarred face that contrasted with the youthful limbs. When he saw Daisy, he laughed derisively, knowing she couldn't stop him, and turned to push again.

Daisy's heart hammered wildly. That cart was all she had left; it would be close to impossible to sell her wares and move Fannie around the city without it. She rushed forward a few steps. "Stop!" she shouted again.

The boys ignored her, and her cart was being dragged away from her. Daisy had to stop it. With a yell of rage, she rushed forward, her small hands bunched into bony fists, and pounded both of them down into the bigger boy's back. He jumped back, roaring with surprise; Daisy screeched, letting out a scything kick at his feet. Her toe painfully met something hard, and the big boy bent over, screaming.

"Oi!" shouted the smaller boy, the one who'd been pulling. "Stop it!"

Daisy whirled around, and the boy was holding up a makeshift knife – a piece of jagged glass, one end wrapped in cloth to make a handle. The edge flashed dreadfully, catching a golden fragment of firelight. She faltered, but Fannie was screaming and crying behind her, and she couldn't let go of the cart.

"Go away!" she shrieked, rushing at the smaller boy, her arms windmilling wildly as though she was shooing away an aggressive gander. "Leave us alone!"

He swiped, madly, in her direction with the knife; she avoided him and somehow landed a wild blow on his face, making him scream and stagger back. When he flailed with the knife again, Daisy wasn't quick enough, and she felt the ripping of skin along her forearm. She stumbled back, crying out in agony, grasping at her arm, hot blood slick between her fingers.

Footsteps crunched behind her, and Daisy whipped around just as the big boy let out a swinging punch toward her face. It missed, grazing narrowly along her shoulder, and Daisy flung herself against him at the moment when he was off balance. They were rolling over each other, his weight crushing her, his hands grappling for her throat, her nails clawing at his eyes, and she pulled up her knees and drove them both as hard as she could into his groin. The big boy squealed like a scared pig. He flung her away, scrambling to his feet, and bolted.

"No!" shrieked Fannie's voice. "No!"

"Ahh!" roared the smaller boy, in pain.

Daisy sat up, breathless, bleeding, and the smaller boy was right above her, his glass knife held high, ready for a fatal blow. But before he could deal it, Fannie was beside her. She seized the boy's free hand and bit down, hard, on two of his fingers. The glass tumbled from his grip, and he let out a wild kick in Fannie's direction. She was flung backwards, rolling across the riverbank, her cries of pain ripping through Daisy's heart.

"Fannie. Fannie!" Daisy scrabbled after her daughter, who was a sobbing heap amid thick mud and straggly grass. She pulled Fannie into her lap, turning her so that the firelight fell on her, her hands rushing over the child's face, limbs, chest. Fannie was screaming and crying, and Daisy found a patch of sticky blood at her hairline, where her head had struck a stone.

"I'm so sorry. I'm so sorry, darling." Daisy's breath came in broken, sobbing chunks. "I'm so sorry." She clutched Fannie close to her, faintly reassured by the strength in the child's arms when she wrapped them around Daisy's neck and clung to her.

It was a long few minutes before Fannie's sobs began to abate, and Daisy's panicked mind could slow down to the point where she was able to look around. To her shock, the cart was still there, lying on its side a few feet away. She must have frightened off the boys enough that they abandoned it, but at what cost? Blood was still oozing from the wound in her arm, and when she carried Fannie over to the firelight, a great lump was forming on the little girl's head. At least, when she set Fannie down on her feet, the three-year-old hurried over to the blanket and wrapped it around her with no sign of trouble.

She needed to bathe their wounds. Daisy's body ached with exhaustion after the long day and the terrible fight, but she'd seen what happened to wounds on the street, seen the bloated green-and-black limbs that rotted while their owners yet lived. Retrieving a broken piece of pottery from the cart, she carried it down to the river and scooped up some dirty, frigid water, then used the hem of her dress to clean the graze on Fannie's forehead. It had already stopped bleeding. She tore a piece from her sleeve and bound it up, and the little girl laid herself down and slept, the grubby cloth tied pitifully around her head.

Bathing her own wound was far more difficult. For a start, every touch of the rough, damp cloth against her torn skin made her want to scream. The blood wouldn't stop coming; every time she cleaned it away, more seeped out, and the sight and the metallic smell of it made her stomach turn. She gave up trying to stop the bleeding at length, tore off another piece of her dress, and wrapped it awkwardly around her arm. It was impossible to tie off the bandage with one hand, so she tucked it in as best as she could and hoped it would stay in place.

She supposed she should move the cart. But where? And how? And why wake Fannie, when she was sleeping so soundly? Daisy didn't suppose those boys would be back, and besides, it seemed as though this city was filled with people who wanted to hurt her. Jack had been right. She should have moved with him.

Too tired to contemplate any further, Daisy lay down beside Fannie, curling herself around the child against the warmth of the dying fire. And though her body was exhausted, she kept hearing footsteps on the riverbank, voices in the night, and it was a long, long time before sleep came for her.

A FAMILIAR, plucking motion dragged Daisy from the depths of sleep. Fannie wanted something. She always tugged at Daisy's sleeve like this when she lay in bed beside Bart, his arm draped over her, their hands wrapped together, her free arm hanging over the side of the bed.

Fannie tugged again. Daisy mumbled, "Go back to bed, darling," and drew her hand back under the covers, and a stab of searing pain ran through her arm. Her eyes snapped open. There was no bed, no Bart, no cozy tenement, no light, no fire. Just this cold riverbank, with mist hanging low over the surface of the river in choking coldness, and the ashes of a dead fire, and her arm hot and throbbing and so painful that it made nausea churn in her gut.

Fannie! Daisy stirred, frightened, but felt a familiar, comforting weight against her chest. Fannie was curled up tightly against her. She relaxed slightly, burying her burning forehead in Fannie's hair. A clattering of traffic on the bridge above. Nearly morning. But she needed more sleep first. Sleep... just sleep. The waves of pain flowing through her body, originating in her arm, seemed to be driving her deeper and deeper into slumber...

The tugging again, and this time it sent a jab of agony through her when she snatched her arm away, wrapping them both tightly around Fannie. Her eyes fluttered open, and it wasn't Fannie standing beside her, tugging at her arm, but the night was filled with the soft sound of a little child crying. Blinking against her exhaustion, Daisy just barely picked out the shape of a small child standing beside her. He could hardly be any older than Fannie. She couldn't see his face, but she could hear him crying and the chatter of his teeth as he shivered.

"Go away," Daisy moaned. "I'm not your mama."

The child's crying intensified, and a small hand fluttered on her arm, delicately avoiding the bandage, crossing over to her other hand and grabbing desperately at her fingers.

Daisy closed her eyes again, ignoring the child. She just wanted to sleep. But his crying was constant and steady, and it had a hauntingly rhythmic quality to it, as though this child had been crying for a very long time and knew he would cry for longer, too. She couldn't sleep with it in her ears, and she just wanted sleep... just wanted to drift away into steady slumber...

It was easiest, then, to just lift the corner of the blanket. Immediately, a small, cold, trembling body pressed itself against her. The child laid his head on Fannie's hip, tucking his body against her own, and Daisy wrapped the blanket around all of them. He lent extra warmth to this freezing night, and in a few moments, pain had driven her back into the welcome arms of sleep.

CHAPTER 7

DAISY WOKE to the kiss of sunlight on her cheek and the bitter throb of agony in her arm. She lay very still, her arms cuddled around Fannie, her chin resting on the top of the child's head. Sunshine... it had been a long time since they'd had real sunshine, even though the spring was now wearing on. She took slow breaths, trying to ignore the insistent pain. Something was nudging at the back of her memory about how that pain came to be, but she pushed it all down. For now, it was enough to lie here with the sun on her face and the gentle pressure of Fannie curled up against her back.

No... that didn't seem right. Fannie was lying in her arms, wasn't she? Why, then, was there also a small figure cuddled up against her back? And Fannie... Fannie! She'd been hurt last night in the struggle.

A jolt of terror stabbed through Daisy's body, and she gasped, her eyes snapping open. Piercing sunlight seared her vision. Groaning, she struggled to blink away the purple after-image and looked down into a completely unfamiliar pair of brown eyes.

"What?" Daisy cried, pushing away from the person in her arms. No. Not person. *Child.* It was a tiny child, and he squealed in shock when she moved, then grabbed at the front of her dress and buried his little face in her chest as though desperate not to be pushed away.

The memory of the child's arrival washed slowly through Daisy's mind. It hadn't seemed real, but the boy was real enough. He was small and trembling, and an unwashed reek rose from his body, bitter and harsh. His hair was long, wild, and caked with streaks of grey mud. And the tiny hands that clutched her dress were all but skeletal. He made poor little Fannie look like a healthy child.

Daisy's revulsion ebbed almost instantly into aching empathy. It was impossible, with the child so cuddled into her arms, to do anything other than to hold him a little closer.

"Where did you come from?" she murmured.

Her voice woke Fannie, who, to Daisy's tremendous relief, sat up abruptly and pushed their small blanket down. When Daisy craned her neck to look back at her, the little girl's eyes were gloriously bright and curious. She reached over Daisy and gave the little boy a gentle poke with her finger.

"Who this, Mama?" she asked.

"I don't know, darling." Daisy brushed some of the boy's stiff, filthy hair away from his face. "What's your name, little one?"

The boy let out a despairing whimper and clung to her more tightly.

"Afraid," Fannie observed.

"Yes, my love. He's afraid." He had reason to be, Daisy reflected; judging by the looks of him, he'd been alone for a long time.

She wanted to sit up and stoke the fire, warm the boy's shivering frame, but when she stirred another wave of agony ran through her arm, forcing her to fall back with a moan. She extricated her arm from under the boy and carefully explored her wounded arm and makeshift bandage with her free hand. It was almost too unbearable to touch the bandage even with the lightest pressure of her fingertips, and the skin at the edges of the bandage was reddened and hot to the touch.

She sagged back against the cold dirt with a moan.

"Who are you?" Fannie asked the boy loudly.

He clung to Daisy all the tighter, letting out another panicked whimper that held deep and incessant fear, the kind of fear that a child his age should never have experienced, but that seemed an essential part of the boy's being.

Daisy wrapped her arms around him again, but the movement was automatic. She knew she needed to get rid of this boy as quickly as she could. Should she push him away, and ignore him? The thought was terrible; she imagined him following her, crying and pleading, and her heart trembled within her.

No, she would have to take him to the one place that she had hoped never to go. The one place that was even worse than the streets.

❧

DAISY HAD SLEPT FAR LONGER than she usually did. The sun was high in the sky as she set off, tugging the handcart out from beneath the bridge even though every step she took sent a fresh lance of pain through her wounded arm. Fannie stood in the cart, clutching at the edge, leaning over it to stare down at the little boy. He toddled beside Daisy, clinging to her skirt with one hand. Even though he had to be older than Fannie – maybe four – he had his filthy thumb in his mouth, and sucked it persistently, staring up at Daisy from time to time out of great dark eyes whose lashes were sparkling with tears.

She tried not to look into his eyes when he did so. She feared she would lose herself in them.

With the park at her back, Daisy dragged the cart through the streets, groaning with pain over every bump and pothole. Fannie kept throwing herself against the side of the cart, reaching toward the boy, squealing and laughing. The boy shrank back from her each time, as though fearing that her tiny daughter would somehow hurt him. She tried not to think about what must have happened to this child to make him so afraid. She tried not to think about anything other than moving each foot, one at a time, driving herself forward, the hunger gnawing at her gut.

In the back of her mind, she thought of Jack, and wondered if he had fixed up those books as he'd promised. The knowledge that he would be waiting for her at the edge of the park when she returned was the only thing that kept her moving forward, that gave her any hope for this day.

That hope felt immediately and completely snuffed out when she reached her destination.

It had been years since the last time that Daisy had laid eyes on the workhouse. Four years, in fact, since the day Bart had proposed, had swept her away, had taken her off into a glorious new life that she had never dared to imagine for herself. The memories of those blissful few years – their wedding day, their new home, their baby – were enough to make tears sting the back of her eyes.

Even if a thousand years passed between the last time she'd seen the workhouse and the next, it would not be long enough.

The building was the model of utter austerity and grim bleakness. Its walls rose sheer and unyielding in front of her, a vast thing, towering like a dictator over the humbler buildings that huddled around it as though bowing in terrified obeisance. There was no garden. There was just a high wall, topped with metal spikes, and a great wrought-iron gate across the street from where Daisy stood with the cart and the children. Beyond, the wall of the workhouse, its windows slits, staring like eyes that could never close, that could never rest.

She knew that those windows hardly let in any light, much less warmth. She knew the way those rooms smelled. Cheap soap and gruel. Bland, tasteless, heartless smells, so different from the cream and salt and butter and meat and perfume and flowers that had filled the air in the little tenement where Daisy had once been happy. She took a deep breath, fancying she could smell that bleak workhouse right at this moment, and the phantom scent awakened a myriad of memories crowding around her like a black tide that could drown her at any moment: the bullying and the beatings, the starvation, the cold hard benches in the schoolroom where no one had listened or learned anything, the windowless refractory ward that was so dark one began to doubt one's own existence after a few hours of solitary confinement for even the tiniest infraction...

She turned away with a shuddering gasp of horror, as though she could evade the memories. Daisy had never known anything other than the workhouse and Bart. She had been born there. And if she walked up to those doors, detangled the boy's tiny claw from her skirt, and thrust him into the arms of the waiting porter, this was the fate to which she would condemn him. Daisy had considered it a fate worse than death.

Feeling the pressure of eyes upon her, Daisy looked down. The boy was staring up at her. His eyes were deep and limpid, and they held something far worse than fear: Trust. He trusted her. Alone, hungry, scared, and unloved, he had come up to her, of all people, in the night.

She realised, with a sickening wave of certainty, that she could not let him go into this dreadful place. Not even for Fannie. That made her a terrible mother, she thought, but it was a simple fact, and the throbbing in her arm and the agony in her feet and the hunger in her belly all were far worse than the sick knowledge of her guilt. She did not have the strength for her own shame.

"Well, I suppose we'd better go and meet Jack by the park," she said, her voice as feeble and cracked as her heart felt.

"Mama, I hungry," said Fannie faintly.

"I'll find us some food soon, darling," said Daisy. She reached over and allowed herself to ruffle a hand through the filthy hair of the boy. "For you, too," she added, meaning it, even though she had no idea how she was going to feed two children when she had been struggling for a year to keep only one alive.

The boy opened his mouth and spoke for the first time.

"I'm Sam," he said.

"Well, hello there, Sam," said Daisy. "We're going to take care of you. Don't you worry."

She was the one who was going to worry.

THE TREK back to the park had felt long and laborious, even though it was only a few blocks, and the afternoon was slipping away by the time Daisy reached it. Fannie had helped her to scrounge a few bits of useful rubbish along the way: some string, an old, stained bonnet, a cracked wooden bowl that could still hold solids. Daisy would have given anything for that bowl to be filled with even the weakest gruel. Her arm ached incessantly, and Fannie was beginning to fuss and whimper with hunger.

But the thought of Jack pulled her on, and she walked with Sam's hand in her own until he began to cry quietly from exhaustion; then she lifted Sam into the cart with Fannie, to her child's delight, and pulled them both. When they reached the line of peddlers around the park, their cries rising through the hectic bustle of the late-afternoon streets, Daisy's eyes swept the street for Jack. She scanned every face in the crowd as she maneuvered her cart into its spot. She had been expecting to see him in his old spot beside hers, but there was no sign of him.

"Where Jack?" asked Fannie.

"Jack?" said Sam.

"A nice man, who helps us sometimes," said Daisy.

"Mama's friend," Fannie informed him.

More than that, thought Daisy, but was he? It was one thing to know she loved him; whether or not he loved her back was quite another. It had already seemed so impossible that she could earn the love of a man like Bart once in her lifetime, let alone twice. And the more she looked up and down the street, the more she began to doubt that the kindness in Jack's grey eyes was anything more than simple decency.

They needed those books. The books would feed all three of them for a few days, long enough for Daisy to sell more rubbish and perhaps sew a few coins into her dress again. Perhaps she could even buy a tiny bit of soap and give Sam a wash. She and Fannie tried to clean themselves regularly in the river, but Sam looked as though he hadn't been clean in years.

Jack just had to bring her those books. He would. Of course, he would. Why would he not?

She stared into the street until her eyes burned, watching for him.

JACK DID NOT COME.

It was around four o' clock, with the sun rapidly sinking and the cold creeping up out of the shadows to wrap its frigid fingers around Daisy's bare throat, that she realised he wasn't coming. Fannie grew more and more fussy, whimpering and crying with hunger, and the more Daisy promised they would eat as soon as Jack arrived, the more Fannie fussed.

"Where's Jack?" she howled. "Where's Jack?"

Sam, on the other hand, made no fuss at all. He sat in the bottom of the cart with his small arms wrapped around his legs, not saying anything: a child who knew that crying achieved nothing, and that he would not be heard. Somehow, it was more chilling than Fannie's unhappy whimpers.

"Jack's not coming today, my love," Daisy said at last, uttering the terrible truth that cracked her heart open.

"Why?" Fannie demanded.

"I'm sure he's just busy." Daisy tried her best to believe her own words. "It must have taken him longer to glue those books than he thought it would."

She remembered his cough yesterday, and a chill ran through her bones. A corner of her heart had begun to wonder if Jack had taken those books and disappeared. But why would he? He had shared his food with them so often. He would never steal from her.

The other possibility, however, was so much worse. Jack had become a pinprick of light in Daisy's dark world and losing him once had been hard enough. To lose him twice...

"Where's Jack?" Fannie shrieked. "I hungry."

Daisy couldn't bear for the child to spend the whole night screaming again. Leaning on the cart with her good arm, trying to ignore the throb of her wound, she smiled at the little girl. "Maybe he'll be here later. Let's sing until he does."

Fannie stared at her, a tiny smile returning to her lips, and clapped her hands.

Daisy seldom sang anymore these days. She had sung to Fannie all the time when she was little, but since she lost Bart, it had seemed impossible to coax a melody from her dry and shrivelled heart. Now, she was desperate, and she found the words somewhere and sang them quietly.

"Hush, little baby, don't say a word," she sang. "Mama's going to buy you a mockingbird."

"Bird," Fannie breathed, leaning back against the cart, her head on Sam's shoulder. Sam glanced at her as though surprised, but his eyes quickly returned to Daisy, and he seemed to be listening with rapt attention. Neither of them showed any sign of falling asleep, but at least they were quiet and listening.

Daisy kept singing, her eyes returning to the street in a last despairing bid to find Jack, but what she saw instead surprised her. A portly woman with a shopping basket on her arm had stopped near Daisy and was listening, a faint smile on her face. It was so odd for a stranger to smile at her that Daisy faltered for a second, worried that the woman was going to hurt her somehow, but Fannie's silence kept her going. After a few moments, the woman moved on.

It was just a few notes later that a young man stopped, listening, and he seemed pleased by the sound of her voice, too.

An idea formed in Daisy's mind, although something about it saddened her. She glanced down at the children, reaching the end of the lullaby. The thought of what she had to do sickened her. Bart would hate this... but he would hate for Fannie to starve tonight even more.

"Fannie," Daisy said, "would you like to help Mama?"

Fannie sat up. "I help," she said proudly.

Sam looked up at her with his soft eyes. "Me, too."

"Wonderful." Daisy forced a smile, lifting the two children out of the cart one at a time. The wind was chill, so she took the blanket from where it was folded in the bottom of the cart as well and wrapped it around their shoulders. "I'm going to sing for these nice people passing by, and they'll want to give us money," she told the children, tucking the blanket in nicely. "But I don't have a cup for the money, so your hands must be the cups, all right?"

"Like this?" asked Sam, extending a small hand in a practiced manner that broke Daisy's heart. This child had begged before. Fannie glanced at him, giggled, and did the same.

"Just like that," she said, and though the sight of her child on the pavement with a hand outstretched made her heart burn, a more calculating part of her was pleased with the effect. Grubby though they were, they were both beautiful children. Surely, they would stir people's hearts toward them.

She took up her spot behind them again and cleared her throat, willing her voice to come back to life. Then she began to sing "Amazing Grace".

A wretch like me. She could only hope that there was a little grace to spare for her in the world, and a few moments later, when someone dropped a sixpence into Fannie's outstretched hand, her voice gained a little strength. Maybe they would survive this latest crisis, after all.

Even without Jack.

JACK'S HEAD was filled with a sharp, panging agony that took his breath away. He managed only little gasps of air as he lay on some cold, hard surface, the patter of rain on his face, his limbs shivering with cold. Each shudder sent a fresh pang of pain through his head.

Rain... it soaked into his clothes, beat against his skin. But there was something more sinister about it. Jack tried to remember but thinking made his head sting sharply. He groaned and rolled over, groping for his blanket. His fingers found the edge, and it tore away in his fingers like paper.

Paper. Daisy's books. Her books. They'd be soaked.

Jack sat up, a sharp movement that caused him so much pain that he cried aloud, clutching at his head. His hands were covered in something wet, clingy. Printed paper. The books.

"No, no," Jack gasped. "No."

He looked around for his cart even though every moment made his head sting more sharply, but everything was wrong. He wasn't in his snug little alleyway. He was on the street. It was very dark, and the rain was coming down in sheets, a shimmering curtain in the light of the nearest streetlamp. The streets were all but empty. Where was he? Why was he lying here?

His cart lay beside him, and the sight of it seemed to jog a memory, distant and painful. The cart was lying on its side, one wheel in the air; the other had been smashed into matchsticks and lay scattered across the pavement and in the street itself.

"No," Jack gasped. His cart was all he had. He tried to get up but could force himself only to his knees before the pain jabbed through his body, sending lurching nausea into his throat. Collapsing to his hands and knees, he vomited into the gutter, then fell back to his side, clutching his head, trembling and gasping. He was reduced to a shuddering heap of agony.

His memory was coming back in fragments. Pushing the cart... this much he remembered. He had Daisy's books with him... he was going to give them to her... it was busy, the street loud with horses and carriages, the pavement crowded with people who cursed and shoved at him as he struggled through with the cart...

The books. He needed to find those books. Struggling once again to his hands and knees, he crawled over to the ruined cart, noticing dully the bloodied handprints he left on the pavement; he could feel the warm trickle of blood across his scalp. Reaching the cart, he grunted with effort, turning it over.

Daisy's books lay in a puddle, soaked through. Their freshly glued bindings were torn away, and when he gingerly lifted one from the puddle, he saw that some of its pages were badly torn.

Tears stung the back of Jack's eyes. What had he done? These books were all that Daisy had with which to feed Fannie. And they were the only thing he had that he could do for her, that he could do to show her how much he loved her.

Now, they were ruined. Jack had ruined them.

He tried, again, to think what had happened. The busy street. There had been another peddler on the corner just up ahead, selling fish. Jack's cart couldn't fit around it on the pavement, so he had to cross the street. He had pulled the cart into the road, heard the warning shouts, looked up to see the out-of-control hansom cab galloping toward him...

Darkness, impact, and then nothing. And now this.

Jack buried his face in his hands, a sob wrenching free of his throat before he could stop it. Daisy was out there in the darkness and the rain, thinking that he had stolen her books from her. She must think he was the worst kind of thief, the worst kind of traitor.

And she and Fannie would go hungry tonight.

Jack sagged back onto the pavement with a rustle of paper. Someone had covered him in newspapers, he realised; they were soaked through now, and had disintegrated into a sticky mess. A small and unlikely kindness. He cupped his throbbing head in a freezing hand.

He had no idea what he was going to do now. His spinning head was already driving him back toward unconsciousness, even though he could feel the burning in his chest grow worse as he lay here in the cold rain. Perhaps this really was the end. Perhaps he would die, and Daisy would never know that he loved her.

He clung to the memory of her beautiful, wide eyes, her sudden smile when she saw him. She was the one lovely thing he had ever had in his life.

And if this was his dying moment, he would use it to think about her.

PART III

CHAPTER 8

Two Years Later

THERE WERE times when Daisy wondered if she had made the right decision to bring her children to this tenement. In some ways, the street had been better.

She tried to ignore the constant, wailing cry of the baby belonging to the family who shared the diminutive space with her. With Fannie bundled up in her arms and Sam curled up close to her back, Daisy kept her eyes tightly shut, her blanket pulled up to her chin. The pallet was hard and uncomfortable, although at least the wood was a little warmer than the ground outside would be.

The baby cried and cried and cried. Its mother, Pauline, did not stir. Daisy wondered if she was still asleep or simply could not bring herself to care. Her six other children were still asleep; Pauline herself would not rise until noon. Daisy knew that Pauline left the house at six in the evenings and only returned in the small hours of the morning, and the fact that all of her children looked profoundly different made it quite clear where it was that she was going.

She pulled the blanket up to cover her nose, blocking out the unwashed stench of the other children and the smoky atmosphere of the tenement. The fire in the middle of the floor had gone out, but smoke still lingered against the ceiling, which was simply composed of the bare wooden floorboards of the level above.

Sleep did not come, but at length, sunlight did; there were no windows in this tiny room, but sunlight pierced the holes in the wall where mortar had crumbled away into dust, and it touched Fannie's hair in a way that made it sparkle just a little in its red-gold way. Daisy sat up, stirred to action, and touched Fannie's shoulder. Her movement woke Sam in an instant.

"Good morning, my darlings," said Daisy. She propped her back against the cold, draft wall and smiled at them, a surge of love momentarily drowning out the cries of the baby and the smokiness of the air. Fannie sat up and tumbled immediately into Daisy's lap, burrowing against her stomach into a little ball of warmth. Sam was a little more reserved, but he still squeezed himself close against Daisy, resting his tousled little head on her shoulder. She ran a hand through his short hair. She had shorn it all last summer, when lice had infested both children; Fannie's had grown fast, but not Sam's.

"Morning, Mama." Fannie looked up at her with angelic eyes. "I love you."

"Oh, darling, I love you too." Daisy kissed her forehead.

Pauline sat up and let out a deep, guttural, viper hiss. "Shut up!" she snarled. "I'm tired."

Her own children sat up, shaking their heads in consternation, whimpering. The baby's cries continued. Pauline pulled her blanket over her head and slept on.

Daisy couldn't stand the sound of that poor baby for a moment longer. There was little point staying here in the tenement, in any case; sunshine made the rich more generous, and she needed all of their generosity.

"Come on," she whispered to Fannie and Sam. "Let's get up."

She retrieved a flannel and small, slightly leaky basin from beside their sleeping pallet, representing almost all of her material wealth in this world, and splashed some cold water into the basin from the bucket in the corner. Using the flannel, she washed the children's faces and smoothed down her hair as best and quickly as she could, aware of the water leaking out into the already-rotten wooden floor. Shushing Fannie's protests, she straightened out their clothes. They slept in them; with their only blanket as threadbare as it was, Daisy had no other choice, but people seemed to be kinder to children who had clean faces and whose clothes were not so badly wrinkled.

By the time they left the tenement and hurried down a wobbling staircase to the front door, Pauline had hissed at them twice more, still ignoring the baby. It was a blissful relief to step outside and look up at a blue, blue sky. It was April, and Daisy could feel the first stirrings of spring around them; this was the first nice day in a while. That reality reminded her of why she bothered with putting up with Pauline and paying their rent in the first place. Even this was better than sleeping under bridges or under the cart she'd sold long ago.

She lifted her skirts a little, ostensibly to step over a muddy puddle, but really feeling the reassuring weight of the coins sewn into the hem. Somehow, she'd managed to cling to the money for the cart, and even added to it a little in the intervening months. One day, she would have a tenement of her own – a tiny place, to be sure, perhaps even poorer than the one she had now, but one without Pauline and her starving children, whom she habitually sold as soon as they turned six or seven years old and could be useful to some chimney-sweep or shopkeeper.

"Where are we going today, Mama?" asked Fannie, clutching her hand.

Daisy led them on through the dreadful slums that surrounded them; the stray animals picking through rubbish that had long since been cleaned of every edible morsel by desperate human souls; the tattered shelters of rags and sticks; the muddied streets, scattered with scraps of filth.

"I think we'll try going a little further south today," said Daisy.

"It's far to walk," said Sam. There was no protest in his voice, only a question.

"I know, but we haven't been there before," Daisy told him.

Fannie's eyes brightened. "Maybe we'll find Jack."

"Maybe," said Daisy, allowing the hope in Fannie's eyes to ignite a similar tiny spark in her own.

"Our last spot was good," said Sam, sounding faintly disappointed.

"But Jack wasn't there," said Fannie. "We keep going around to find Jack."

It had been a crazy idea, Daisy admitted to herself, as she walked on with a child's hand in each of her own. The park had been a decent enough spot, and she'd stayed there for months, hoping Jack would return. When he didn't, all she had been able to think of doing was to search for him; singing made this easier. But that winter, she'd given up. She'd hired the tenement and stayed closer to it.

Fannie was the one who wouldn't give up. She skipped along beside Daisy with an energy she envied. "Today, we find Jack," she said, with determination.

"Maybe," Daisy said again.

She tried to hope, tried to feel the same fervor as Fannie did. She couldn't bring herself to tell Fannie what she both knew and feared was true: Jack was long dead.

DAISY CLOSED her eyes and pitched her voice a little higher, giving it the ringing, almost heavenly quality that rich people liked.

"All things bright and beautiful, all creatures great and small," she sang. "All things wise and wonderful, the Lord God made them all."

There was a clink of money, and Daisy half-opened one eye, glancing down at where Fannie and Sam knelt in front of her with their hands out in the now-familiar pose she still hated. Someone had dropped a few pennies into Sam's hand; he closed it and thanked them quickly, and Fannie gave them a winning smile for good measure.

They knew the sick routine all too well. Daisy struggled to keep her voice from faltering at the thought of what Bart would think of her if he saw their daughter kneeling on the street. If he saw the dreadful brown calluses on his daughter's knees. But what else could she do? She knew one thing for sure, he would never have resented her for taking in Sam. He would have loved Sam as his own child, the way she loved him.

"He gave us eyes to see them, and lips that we might tell how great is God Almighty, Who made all things well." Daisy held the last note for an extra second and was rewarded as a tuppence tumbled into Sam's palm. The man who threw the tuppence gave her a quick, searching look that she hated, but it seemed that hunger had taken all of the curves that men liked, and he hastened on.

She let out a long breath and sipped dirty water from a cup, sharing it with the children. They had made enough for bread; this afternoon, they'd need to make enough for rent. Daisy had learned not to sing for too long. Her voice couldn't hold it.

"Mama," said Fannie, draining the last of the cup, "can I go ask about Jack?"

"Please may I go ask about Jack," Daisy corrected. Bart had been determined that Fannie be well educated, and this felt like the only chance Daisy had to live up to his hopes.

"Please may I go ask about Jack?" Fannie repeated.

"Yes, you may. But don't go where I can't see you," Daisy reminded her.

"Thank you, Mama." Fannie took Daisy's hand and gave it a fat, childish kiss. Then she grabbed Sam's hand and the two of them ran off. It did Daisy's heart good to hear Sam's giggle, but she wondered how much longer she should allow Fannie to keep up with this pointless charade. She'd first started asking people on the street if they'd seen Jack about a year ago, when Daisy had still held a tiny scrap of hope that she would see the grey-eyed peddler again. Now, Daisy didn't know how to stop her, how to tell her Jack was dead.

Or, worse, that he didn't love them.

She sat down on the edge of a fountain and watched closely as Fannie and Sam scampered up to an old woman selling flowers from a handcart in the corner. She listened to them – which wasn't unusual; it seemed Sam's soft eyes could persuade even the cruellest of folks to listen – and then shook her head. Shop by shop, handcart by handcart, stall by stall, the children made their way around the market square where Daisy had chosen to sing, often glancing back to make sure they could still see her.

Daisy took another sip of water and cleared her throat, testing it. The children had almost reached the fountain again; when they did, she would start singing. On Sundays, sometimes she had taken to sitting at the door of a nearby church to pick up some new hymns. She was too ragged for the people to let her inside, but it was good sometimes to sit outside in the fresh air and listen to the words trickling out of the stained-glass windows. They held a ring of truth that sustained her soul even if the people who professed to believe in them so often acted as though the opposite were true.

Fannie's piping voice carried across the cobbled square to Daisy. Daisy could easily see how she was talking to a bent old man with a handcart, selling fish. "We're looking for a man," she was saying earnestly. "A bit taller than you. Dark hair, and grey eyes. Like mine." She widened them, as if for emphasis.

The man leaned over the cart. Sam flinched, tugging Fannie back a step, as if to protect her. Daisy wondered how much of his previous life he remembered. The old man looked friendly enough, and she expected him to say the same things everyone always said: "No, I'm sorry." "How d'you expect to find a single man in all London?" "Where did you last see him?" or, worst of all, "*When* did you last see him?"

When they heard that this mystery man had been gone for two years, they all shook their heads. Some went as far as saying that a man gone for so long didn't want to be found. Fannie never seemed to listen.

But this old man said none of those things. Instead, "Pale grey – very pale?"

Daisy's head snapped up.

"Yes, I think so," said Fannie.

The old man sucked his teeth thoughtfully. "And what did he do for a living?"

Fannie looked helplessly over at Daisy. Suddenly, Daisy's aching feet felt light and soft. She was on her feet and walking across the square, her heart thundering wildly in her ears as though she did still have some hope after all, even if she didn't want to, even if she knew that such hope only led to dismay.

"He mended chairs and peddled them, sir," she said. "Jack Honor was his name."

The old man scratched his white head. "Well, I didn't hear his name, but there was a young man that sounded like him walking through this square last week," he said. "Pullin' a handcart with a few old chairs on it."

Daisy's heart stuttered.

"Jack!" said Fannie. Sam was wide-eyed.

"Sir," Daisy managed, "do you remember where he went?"

"I couldn't tell you, luv," said the old man. "I didn't ask. He sold a few chairs and went on his way. Seemed a really nice young feller, though. Helped me out when a drunk man tried to steal some fish."

It sounded like Jack. Daisy blinked back tears. "Oh, sir, you didn't hear him say anything – anything, that could help us find him?"

The old man looked genuinely troubled. "I'm sorry, lass. He didn't say much. But if you're looking for him, look for the book seller."

Her heart skipped in her chest. "Book seller?"

"Yes, that's all he really said. He was looking for a used book seller. He'd mended some books for her and wanted to find her."

Daisy managed to hold it together for long enough to tell the old man, "Thank you very much," before turning and walking away, covering her mouth with both hands. A sob ripped through her body, then another, and another.

"Mama?" Fannie's little voice was terrified. She tugged at Daisy's sleeve. "Mama, what's wrong?"

"Nothing, darling. Nothing. Mama's just relieved," Daisy choked out between sobs.

Relieved wasn't the right word. Jack was still alive. And more than that, Jack was looking for her, wanting to give her those books even after all this time.

Daisy was more than relieved. For the first time in years, Daisy had hope again.

❧

RAIN DRUMMED on the roof of the tenement, somewhere far above, through several floors of abject poverty. Daisy could hear it only dimly, but she could clearly see the drips running down the inside of the wall, leaving black stains and blossoms of dark mould. She shuddered at the sight of it as she washed the children's faces. All the same, she was nervous about this day. They would have to find an overhang under which she could sing if she didn't want the children to fall ill.

It had been raining for four days, ever since Daisy had first heard about Jack. She and the children had walked to the square every day since, the rain bucketing down on their heads, but Jack had not come back yet. He would, though. Daisy had to believe that he would.

She finished washing Fannie's face and wrung out the flannel in the basin, then turned to little Sam. He was standing very still, his head hanging, and when Daisy raised the flannel, she had to ask him twice to look up.

"Sorry," he mumbled, raising his head.

Daisy's breath caught. Sam's cheeks were red and flushed, unnaturally so.

"Sam, darling, are you all right?" Daisy asked. The child had always had a slight rattle in his breathing, born of years of hardship on the street, but now that she looked at him, the rattle seemed louder than usual.

"Yes," said Sam, the way he always did.

Daisy rested the back of her hand on his forehead and found it painfully hot to the touch. She swallowed her terror, forcing a smile and cursing herself inwardly. Why had she dragged the children out there in the rain in the feeble hope of finding

Jack? She should have stayed closer to home. She should have taken better care of him.

"You're a little warm this morning, darling," she said. "I think you'd better stay home."

"Home?" Sam's eyes widened, and he reached out and clutched Daisy's sleeve with an iron grip.

Daisy gazed at him, her heart melting. This poor child had been abandoned too many times before. She wrapped her arms around him and kissed the burning forehead, and terror curdled in her belly. She needed to find a doctor and medicine, and for that she needed money. She needed to hurry.

"You won't be all alone," she said. "Fannie will be here to keep you company, won't you, darling?"

Fannie smiled, clearly pleased at the prospect of a day at home instead of going out in the rain. She reached out and took Sam's hand. "We can stay home together."

Sam relaxed fractionally. "All right," he said.

"I'll get some tea and come back before noon," Daisy promised. "And then I'll go out again for a little while before dark."

She kissed them both and headed out into the rain. Plodding through the mud, feeling the dampness soak through the cracked soles of her shoes, she paused at the crossroads and gazed longingly down the road that led to the south and to the marketplace where Jack had been. Perhaps today would be the day that she found him...

She took a deep breath, turning around. No. She needed to make as much money as she could and stay close to the tenement.

It was time to give up, once and for all.

She headed north.

CHAPTER 9

DAISY'S BONES hurt as she plodded up the staircase toward the tenement. Her hunger had become weakness; the terrible pangs that had assailed her stomach for the first two days she'd gone without food had abated, as though her body had realised that its agonies would not drive her to eat. Instead, she felt now the simple weakness of a body that had nothing left with which to fuel itself. Dark spots swarmed in the corners of her vision if she moved or turned too fast.

But at last, after paying the rent and buying fresh food for Sam and Fannie every day, she had managed to get her hands on a bottle of medicine. Laudanum. The man at the apothecary had said it would work, and finally break poor Sam's fever. She clutched the precious, expensive glass bottle tightly in both hands, wrapped in a cloth so that no one in the tenement would see it; she had seen the people who injected themselves with opium or drank laudanum like milk, and she was terrified of what they might do to her or to her children to get their hands on it.

Forcing cheerfulness into her voice, Daisy pushed open the tenement door. Pauline's children were sitting on their pallet; the two biggest picked their teeth with their fingernails. Sam and Fannie were in the far corner, huddled together under their blanket.

"Hello, darlings," she said. "I'm home – and look what I've brought."

With a conjurer's flourish, she produced two apples from the bag over her shoulder. They were good apples, too, not mouldy or mealy, but fat and juicy and red. Sam had been refusing food for more than a day now, but surely these would tempt him.

But Sam simply looked up listlessly, then leaned his head back against the wall and screwed his eyes tightly shut again.

Daisy's heart squeezed in her chest. She prayed she'd bought the laudanum in time. Fannie, at least, was sitting up, her eyes very bright and locked on the apples, but she didn't get up and run over to Daisy the way she always used to.

"Fannie, darling, what's the matter?" Daisy approached the children, setting down the apples on the pallet.

Fannie didn't respond. She just lunged forward, seized one of the apples, and began to eat it in great, crunching mouthfuls. Daisy stared at her. Fannie was eating as though she hadn't seen food in days, but she'd had bread that same morning, perhaps even her fill of bread; Sam hadn't wanted his.

"Fannie," she repeated, shocked.

The girl stared up at her, cheeks bulging, apple juice running down her lip. Daisy let out a breath. Well, if Fannie was this hungry, clearly she was healthy enough. So far, whatever Sam had, he hadn't spread it to Fannie.

"Never mind, dear," she said.

Fannie went on devouring the apple, and Daisy un-stoppered the medicine bottle. "Here, Sam," she said. "I've brought you some medicine. It'll do you plenty of good." She kept her voice low, shielding the bottle from Pauline's children with her body; she didn't want them to see it and tell their mother about it.

Sam looked at her with listless eyes. "I'm not hungry," he whispered.

It was an alien thing to hear from a child's mouth. Daisy was used to their constant, unending hunger, and as much as her soul ached every time they begged her for food, she would give anything now for Sam to tell her he was hungry.

"Well, this will help you to feel hungry," she said. She retrieved one of their two tin spoons from under the pallet and poured some of the dark red liquid into it; it looked like wine, but it smelled strangely sweet. Sam took it willingly, and Daisy touched his forehead. It was still burning.

"This will make you all better," she said.

Fannie was nibbling the last scraps of apple from the stick. "Whose apple is this?" she asked, pointing to the leftover one.

Daisy grabbed it quickly, not trusting the hunger in her daughter's eyes. "This is for Sam, darling. It's going to make him feel better."

"All right," Fannie sighed. She sagged back against the wall, and there was something haunted in her face that worried Daisy.

"Sweetheart, what's wrong?" Daisy asked her. "Why are you so hungry?"

Fannie stared at her for a long moment, then looked away, wrapping a small and bony arm around Sam's shoulders.

"I'm just hungry, Mama," she said.

Daisy stared at her child for a moment longer, sinking onto the pallet beside her. She reached out and pulled both children into her arms and cradled them close.

She could only hope that Fannie was telling the truth. But what else could be making her child hungrier than normal? Was she growing? She'd always been small for her age. Maybe she was just making up for lost time.

That had to be it. Daisy prayed that was it as she closed her eyes and squeezed both the children until it felt as though her heart would burst.

❧

"SLOWLY." The old cobbler's voice was warm and patient. "Take your time."

Jack nodded, keeping his hand as steady as he could on the knife as he slowly cut along the lines he'd drawn on the sheet of leather that lay on the workbench in front of him. His toes curled with concentration, and he took slow breaths to keep his hand from wobbling. The blade sliced neatly down the penciled lines he'd drawn there, marking out the shape of a lady's closed shoe.

"There," said the old man, happily, as Jack lifted the blade and looked down at the neatly cut shape. "Good job, young'un. That's lovely."

"Thank you, sir," said Jack.

The cobbler grinned at him with a mouth full of teeth so misshapen and discoloured that they made his mouth look like a box of loose stones. His bushy brows rose on a forehead as wrinkled as the old leather of the shoes he mended, and his watery eyes were a misty shade of blue. Jack supposed that the little old cobbler was as handsome as a gnarled old goblin.

But the kindness shining in his face was the most appealing thing he'd seen in a very long time.

"You're a good boy," said the cobbler fondly. He patted Jack's shoulder with a hard, twisted hand. "We'll have a bit of chicken tonight. Celebrate your first pair of shoes made all on your own."

"I'm not sure I'll finish them tonight," Jack confessed.

"Rubbish, lad. Your stitching is the fastest I've ever seen. Don't you know that's why I gave you this job in the first place?" The old cobbler laughed contentedly.

"Mr. Tanner," said Jack, softly, "I know full well that you knew nothing about my abilities when you saved my life."

Mr. Tanner's eyes softened, but he turned away. He didn't like to talk about the day when they had first met, and truth be told, Jack didn't like to remember it much himself. He had thought that he would perish.

❧

JACK WAS, in hindsight, exceedingly close to perishing, lying sick and wounded on the pavement with his ruined cart beside him, and he lay there all night and all the next morning.

Crowds filled the pavement, hurrying to work, to school, to *life*. People crossed the street to avoid Jack at first, when there was still room, but as the streets grew busier, some simply skirted around him or stepped over him. Even when he had the strength to raise his head and extend a hand toward passersby, croaking for help, they pretended he didn't exist. A few even barked at him to get out of the way. He crawled into the shelter of a nearby overhang and lay there in the shadows, shivering, waiting for death to come for him, and thinking of Daisy, the only thing that seemed capable of soothing his heartache.

Drifting in and out of consciousness, certain that this was his final hour, Jack flinched when he felt the touch of a hand on his shoulder. But the voice that spoke was gentle. "Now then, young man. What happened to you?"

Jack barely had the strength to whisper. "I was knocked down. Please, leave me. I don't have the strength to get out of the way."

"I won't be leaving you," said the gentle voice. "Is this your cart? And these books?"

Jack's arms tightened around the books that he was holding, and he nodded, regretting it instantly when the movement sent a bolt of pain through his wounded head.

"I'll come back for the cart," said the voice. "For now, you're coming with me."

Not knowing the intentions of his would-be saviour, Jack wanted to resist, but old Mr. Tanner had put his arms around

Jack's torso and pulled him to his feet, giving him no choice but to stagger weakly to the cobbler's shop just down the street. He remembered Mr. Tanner's voice gently encouraging him all the way, even when he felt unable to move another inch, and he remembered the delicious softness of the pile of old fabric upon which the cobbler laid him. After that, darkness, and the long rigors of fever, and through it all, the gentle voice of Mr. Tanner, urging him to keep fighting.

❦

IT HAD BEEN ALMOST two years, now, since Jack had won the fight for his life, and he knew that he owed every minute he had lived since to Mr. Tanner.

"Well, God clearly did know about your abilities, son," said the cobbler uncomfortably, grasping a broken shoe and turning it this way and that to inspect the damage. "This needs to be resoled."

"Why do you say that?" asked Jack.

"Because look at it, boy," said Mr. Tanner. He held up the shoe and pried the cracked sole away from the inner. "It's ruined."

"No, no." Jack smiled. "I mean, why do you say that God knew about my abilities?"

"Well, why else would He bring a little foundling who just happened to be a dab hand when it comes to sewing and weaving to the doorstep of a childless old cobbler?" said Mr.

Tanner peevishly, waggling his enormous brows. "Now stop your chatter and get to work on those shoes."

"I just wanted to thank you," said Jack quietly, turning back to his work.

Mr. Tanner's hand rested briefly on his shoulder again. "It's good to have young hands helping me," he said. "Besides, I didn't have much other use for the back room, did I?"

"It's the first time I've ever had a roof over my head," Jack admitted. It wasn't a truth he was proud of, but he knew Mr. Tanner well enough to know that there was no judgment in the old man.

"Well, if you keep learning and working, maybe you'll have more someday," said Mr. Tanner gruffly. "Now, didn't I tell you to keep working, lad?"

He shuffled out to talk to a customer, leaving Jack alone in the workshop, which smelled deliciously like fresh leather and beeswax. Turning back to the leather sheet, Jack lifted the knife and started tracing the outline of the second shoe. Mr. Tanner had promised him payment for his work on making new shoes, and he already gave Jack room and board, even allowing him three whole meals a day. Jack hadn't been hungry in years, and his chest even seemed to have healed now that he slept warm and dry each night.

His eyes wandered from his work to the two books stacked on the end of the workbench. He had placed them there to remind him of why he would work harder and do better than he had ever done before in his life. Why he would spend every free moment wandering the streets, looking for Daisy.

He was going to find her, and he was going to give her and Fannie the life that they deserved.

DAISY WRUNG out the flannel into the basin, the cool water stinging her freezing hands. She laid the damp flannel on Sam's brow, feeling a fresh pang of worry as she noticed how quickly his burning skin seemed to heat the cold water.

Please, God, she prayed silently. *Let the medicine work. Let his fever break.* She swallowed, trying not to think of how empty the medicine bottle had become. It had been just three days since she'd brought Sam the medicine, and already she had used nearly half of the bottle. Sam seemed better for a few hours after taking his medicine, but the fever always returned.

She had come home a few minutes ago to find him shivering helplessly on the pallet even though Fannie had bundled him in their blanket and lay beside him, hugging him close. "He's so warm, Mama," she said, her eyes very wide. "But he keeps shaking."

"The medicine will help," Daisy told her as she coaxed a spoonful through Sam's semiconscious lips.

Now, she prayed that it was true, that it would do something, her heart breaking as she looked at the little boy. He had grown so thin that his grey skin was stretched tightly over his skull, with sunken hollows around his cheeks and eyes. His short hair was mussed and spiky from tossing on the bed, and the little hand that lay on his chest was all bones.

A sudden, loud crunch behind her made her jump. She whipped around in time to see Fannie gripping a piece of cooked fish with both hands, holding it to her face. The child had just bitten into it, and she took another massive bite, choking the food down.

"Fannie!" Daisy gasped. "You're already had a fish!"

She plucked the fish from Fannie's hands and thrust it back into the brown paper parcel, a wave of dismay washing over her. She had given Fannie one of the two fish she had bought, secretly hoping that perhaps there would be something left over of the second fish for Daisy herself. "This is for Sam and me!" she chided loudly.

Fannie's eyes filled with tears. She fell back against the pallet. "Mama, I'm so hungry."

Daisy's heart ached with bewilderment and anger. "But *why*, darling? I gave you half a loaf of bread this morning. How can you be so hungry you would take Sam's fish now?"

Fannie covered her face with her small hands and began to sob relentlessly. The sound terrified Daisy. She'd never heard her child cry like this, and as she stared at her, she began to realise how thin she had become. The bones of Fannie's wrists flexed awfully against her skin as she sobbed into her hands.

Something was terribly wrong.

Sitting on the pallet beside Fannie, Daisy pulled her into her arms. "Hush, my darling. Hush," she whispered. "It's all right. Mama's here. Mama loves you. Mama will always love you."

Fannie wrapped her thin arms around Daisy's neck and sobbed all the more. Daisy stroked her back, trying to swallow her fear. "It's all right. It's all right. But please, darling, tell me what's going on. Why are you acting so strange?"

"They said – I shouldn't – tell you." Fannie's words were broken up by sobs. "They said – they would – they would – "

"*Who* said, my love?" Daisy asked despairingly.

Fannie raised her head and pointed a trembling finger toward the pallet where Pauline and her children slept. Pauline had taken all of them with her this evening.

"Pauline's children?" Daisy said.

"Yes," Fannie said, burying her face back in Daisy's chest and sobbing all the more.

"Oh, my darling, what have they done to you?" Daisy hugged her tightly. "Tell Mama everything. I won't let anyone hurt you again, I promise."

Fannie sat up, taking deep breaths as she spoke, trying to calm her sobs. "They – they saw that – that you bring us food," she sobbed out. "Their mama doesn't – not always." Tears coursed down her cheeks.

Daisy wiped at them. "I know, darling."

"So they – they started taking – ours. When you – when you leave in the morning, they take our food. And if I try to eat – everything before you go, they beat us. Both of us." Fannie gave a whimpering wail of fear and pain. "They kick us and hit us. So I – I take Sam's food and mine, and I – give it to them. Otherwise, they kick us."

Fury washed over Daisy again, breath-taking as a bucket of cold water. She clutched her child tightly, feeling the same strength and rage flow through her blood with which she had attacked the men who tried to take Fannie and the boys who tried to steal their cart. She still had the knotted scar on her forearm to prove that she would fight with her life when it came to caring for her daughter.

But her anger pulled up short when it ran into the thought of those children whose mother didn't want them and had never loved them, and it dissolved into an exasperated pity. Those children knew no other way of survival. What could she do to stop them from taking Sam's and Fannie's food? There was nothing, except to take the children somewhere else, somewhere far away from Pauline and the evil that followed her like a dark mist.

"It's all right, darling," she murmured, kissing the top of Fannie's head. "Don't you worry about a thing. Those children will never hurt either of you again, and I'm going to make sure you have enough to eat."

"But how, Mama?" Fannie sobbed.

She hugged her child more tightly, looking fearfully at Sam where he took short, harsh breaths on the pallet. Outside, the wind howled, blowing a fresh fistful of rain against the gaps in the wall, tiny bursts of spray touching Daisy's skin through the holes.

"I'm going to take you somewhere else," she said.

"But where?" Fannie wailed.

"Don't worry about that. We'll find a place," said Daisy. "I know we will." And as she spoke, she prayed that her words would come true. They didn't have a cart anymore.

If they ended up on the streets again, she could have just condemned Sam to his death.

CHAPTER 10

DESPITE HIS EMACIATED STATE, Sam seemed to be unrealistically heavy in Daisy's arms. She supported his weight in the crook of her left arm, his legs on either side of her torso, his little head leaning on her shoulders. She wished he would keep a better grip around her neck so that her shoulders might take some of his weight, but he seemed unable to do much more than keep his arms draped feebly over her shoulders.

Grunting with effort, Daisy hoisted the child a little higher on her hip.

"Mama, your hand?" Fannie asked softly.

Daisy looked down into two grey eyes filled with fear, and a small hand extended toward her. She reached out and took it, even though that left the arm around Sam aching all the more with his weight. His little body warmed her even through her clothes, and though the heat was almost pleasant in the face of the cold, airless day, it frightened her.

The fear was all the more motive to keep going, even though every bone in her body ached and no one had bothered to listen to her singing, much less to pay her for it. Why would they? She was walking through the most desolate slum she had ever seen, seeking a tenement, and the money in the hem of her dress was all but spent again. She would be lucky to afford a week's rent – the required deposit – on one of the poorest tenements here.

And she would need to be lucky fast, Daisy knew, because neither she nor the children had eaten a bite yet today, and Sam was burning up against her. The sun was sinking, and cold was creeping up from the streets. She clutched the little boy closer. She had a little medicine left; she and Fannie would simply have to go without food for tonight, but the thought of starving poor, sick Sam appalled her.

Even worse was the thought of sleeping out here in the elements with him. She knew, deep in her bones, that to do so would be to kill him.

With rising desperation, she approached the next door. Her knuckles were already sore from knocking, but she let go of Fannie's hand and pounded on it anyway.

It opened a mere crack, a beady eye glaring out at her. "What do you want?" barked a gruff voice.

"I'm looking to hire a tenement, please," said Daisy. "I have money."

"Got one room."

Daisy looked up at the bleak building that towered over them. Poverty was written loudly across its weathered facade, from the bare brick to the boarded-up windows. It looked even worse than the room she had shared with Pauline.

"How much?" she asked.

"Three shillings a week."

"Three shillings." Daisy gasped. "I... I don't have that much."

"Then leave." The eye withdrew.

"No! Wait." Daisy slammed a hand against the door in desperation. "I have two shillings and sixpence. I could pay you back double next week." It was a reckless thing to say; as it stood, Daisy wasn't sure she could even pay two shillings and sixpence each week.

There was no response. The door simply slammed shut, and the sound of it woke Sam, who suddenly began to cry. The sound was small and shrill, and it chilled Daisy to the bone. She had never heard him cry like this.

"Sam, darling, what's the matter?" She stumbled away from the building, having long since learned that to hang around buildings once one had been rejected invited disaster, and over to a nearby home that seemed abandoned. It was a gaunt thing, hollowed-out, the windows all empty, but it had concrete steps and Daisy sank to her knees, sitting Sam down on them. He reeled where he sat, as though too weak to sit up, and she clutched at his shoulders. "Sam, talk to me," she gasped.

"It hurts, it hurts," Sam sobbed, clutching at his chest. "Everything hurts."

"Oh, darling." Daisy floundered under the weight of her distress for him. She groped in her canvas bag, pulling out the medicine bottle, and poured a spoonful of it with shaking hands. Sam swallowed it slowly, as though his throat hurt, and then continued his small, feeble cry.

Daisy fell to her knees beside him, tears stinging her eyes, and cried out in her heart. She wanted to pray, but the despair in her was too vast for words, so she simply raised up her broken soul toward heaven and hoped against hope that someone would be listening.

There was a long, wooden moan from somewhere in front of them. Daisy threw one arm around Sam and seized Fannie's hand, looking up sharply, ready to run or fight. The building's front door was opening slowly, swinging drunkenly on one hinge, and a tiny little mouse of a woman stepped onto the threshold. Her dress had been mended so many times that it was a faded patchwork; it was impossible to tell which cut or colour it had originally been, and it hung like a sack on her bony frame. Her hair was a wild, tangled grey muss around her head. But there was softness in her eyes, and Daisy paused, staring pleadingly into them.

"What's the matter with the boy?" the woman asked, her voice very gentle.

"I don't know," Daisy admitted, tears stinging her eyes. "He's so sick. My daughter and I haven't gotten anything, but he's just not getting better."

"You asked Mrs. Firkin across the street for a place to live?" The woman's accent was strange, lilting, and soothing in its way.

"I don't have the money." Daisy hung her head.

The woman descended the steps on bare feet; Daisy noticed she was missing both of her little toes, puckered scars left behind where the digits used to be. She knelt down and touched Sam's brow. "Poor mite," she said. "You can't stay out here."

"I don't know where to go," Daisy sobbed.

"Nell?" said a masculine voice, thin and reedy. "We have space."

Daisy and the woman both looked up. The stooped old figure in the doorway was too old to be the woman's husband; his skin hung in folds from his bones, and he shakily clutched a walking stick as gnarled and bent as he was.

"We do have space," said Nell. "It's cold and drafty and mouldy and it's not much, but it's a roof."

Daisy swiped at her tears. "I have – I can pay two shillings a week. Maybe more."

"The place is condemned. We're hiding here," said Nell, "for now. No one's paying for anything. But if we work together, we can get our food a little cheaper." She touched Sam's forehead again.

Daisy stared at her, struggling to comprehend the simple kindness that this woman was showing her. Seeing the suspicion in her eyes, Nell smiled gently.

"We won't hurt you," she said. "And perhaps I can help you with the bairn. I was a nurse once."

"Oh, please." Daisy struggled to hold back her tears. "Please help us."

"We don't have much to give you, but we'll do what we can, lass," said the old man.

"Give me the little one." Nell reached out and scooped Sam into her arms.

A great weight was lifting just a little from Daisy's shoulders, and she followed Nell into the building, and saw at once why it had been condemned. It was little more than a great, hollowed-out shell. The remnants of what must once have been wooden floors forming stories above them now lay in a mad jumble of beams and planks, a great heap of blackened rubble upon the floor. The walls were all covered in soot; there were no windows, and there were gaps in the roof, and everything smelled of acrid smoke.

There was a small clearing in the centre of the building, where rubble had been pushed aside to create a lumpen circle containing a few sleeping mats and the remnants of a cooking fire. Two small children, perhaps six or seven years old, stared up as Nell and the old man approached them, Sam still in Nell's arms. Daisy followed, keeping a good grip on Fannie's hand.

"Delia, Franklin, these people are our friends," said Nell, laying Sam down on one of the mats.

Fannie's hand tightened on Daisy's. Daisy glanced down, expecting to see her child frightened after what Pauline's children had done to her. Instead, Fannie looked eager. She pulled her hand out of Daisy's and ran over to the other children.

"Do you like playing tag?" she asked.

"Oh, they love tag," chuckled the old man. He prodded Fannie lightly in the shoulder. "You're It!"

The children scattered into the ruins, and Daisy sank down beside Sam, resting a hand on him. She looked up at Nell, trying to dispel the tears in her eyes.

"Why are you helping me?" she whispered.

Nell shrugged. "What point is there to scratching for survival if we don't love each other?" she said, and Daisy had no answer to that.

SUNDAY AFTERNOON HAD RENDERED the market square very quiet, slumbering under the weight of a blanket of mist. Jack kept his shoulders hunched against the thick fabric of his coat as he moved down the street. He was beginning to feel that this afternoon's expedition was pointless, but then again, hadn't they all begun to feel pointless? Hadn't he been searching for Daisy for the past two years without finding her?

Her books bumped against his hip in a leather satchel, and Jack shook his head, trying to dispel the hopeless thoughts. She'd be here somewhere, he knew it. At the bottom of the marketplace, a few stallholders tried to ply their trades even on a Sunday, unable to take a day's rest for fear of starvation; perhaps she was among them. He hadn't tried this particular marketplace yet. This might be the day. It was as good a day as any, and besides, if he didn't spend his Sunday afternoons searching for Daisy, what else would he do? Her absence was already enough to drive him mad and distract him even while he was working; it would be a thousand times worse in his idleness.

Smoke from cooking fires hung low over the little square, and as Jack walked into it, he offered a silent prayer of thanks that he no longer found himself working in a place like this. The people behind the ramshackle stalls all had the same broken expressions in their eyes. Their faces were pinched and sallow, and their wares were all variations on meagre and colourless.

Jack went from handcart to handcart, feeling heartbroken at the sorrow in the stallholders' eyes. He knew that sorrow so intimately. The shoes he'd sold hadn't fetched much, but it felt good to have money in his pocket again; he spent a few pennies here and there where he could, trying to bolster the unhappiest faces he saw. Sixpence, however, he had left hidden under his pillow. He would keep on saving and saving until he found her.

He was peering through the smoke of a fire on which a string of gristly sausages was roasting when he spotted the handcart out of the corner of his eye, and its familiar shape sent a jolt of warm rocketing through the length of his body. Whipping around, Jack stared at it. There was no doubt. It was Daisy's. He knew every knot and notch on the wood, every detail of its silhouette, and he stumbled toward it with his heart in his mouth. The slim silhouette behind it had her back turned to him, and he had to try twice before her name would pass through his numb lips.

"Daisy!"

The girl turned around, and disappointment sliced through the length of Jack's body like a blade. She couldn't have been older than thirteen. Too young to be Daisy, much too old to be Fannie.

"I beg your pardon, sir?" she asked.

Jack glanced down at the flowers she was selling from the cart, remembering with a twinge of heartache the wilted poppies Daisy had been trying to sell when he first met her.

"I'm looking for Daisy Parker," he said. "This... this is her handcart."

"No, it is not!" The girl's eyes flared, and she laid both hands possessively on the cart. "I bought it fair and square."

"I'm sure you did, miss," said Jack. "Do you remember the lady you bought it from?"

"Nay, because it was a man," the girl barked at him. "Now unless you're going to buy something, be gone with you."

"I'm sorry." Jack raised both hands in a placating gesture. "I'm sorry."

He doubted that the girl was lying, and that fact made his heart sting within him. If the girl had bought this from someone else, then where had that man gotten it? Had Daisy sold it?

Was Daisy still alive?

The thought that she might not be was unbearable, and Jack turned away sharply as though to escape it. His shoulder collided hard with something soft and yielding, and a middle-aged woman stumbled backward with a cry of horror, holding a large bowl of gruel. It slopped perilously in the bowl, and Jack grabbed it, narrowly keeping it from spilling out.

"Heavens! I'm so sorry," he gasped.

"Oh, that's all right, sir," said the woman, looking up at him. She had refreshingly gentle eyes, enclosed as they were by deep folds of skin; her hair had been dark once, but now fell in messy grey tresses around her shoulders. "No harm done."

Her face was blasted by poverty, and Jack's heart ached for her. She looked so kind. He hoped, if Daisy was still alive, that someone like this woman could be in her life.

"I wonder if I might ask..." he began.

"Hurry up!" called a jovial, reedy old voice. "Getting dark."

The woman looked up, and Jack followed her gaze to where an old man stood at the edge of the square, bent over a stick. He waved a brown paper bag, probably containing bread.

"Ah, wonderful, Papa," called the woman. She gave Jack a brief smile. "I must be going."

He wanted to ask about Daisy, but before he could speak, the old man called out again. "Come along now, Nell."

"Coming, Papa." Nell flashed him a brief smile and hurried away, keeping a firm grip on the gruel.

Jack let her go. He didn't call out after her. What good would it do? He was no closer to finding Daisy than he had ever been.

❦

It was glorious to have some food in her stomach again. Although Daisy feared that she would regret spending a whole shilling of her savings, she felt strengthened now that she had eaten a full bowl of the hot gruel that Nell and her father, Mr. Patrick, had brought from the marketplace. Fannie, too, was sleeping soundly for the first time in days; her cheeks looked at least a little redder now in the light of the small fire that they had made using the charred wood of the rubble.

"Such a precious child, she is," murmured Nell, sitting beside Daisy. The other children were all asleep – Delia and Franklin in a heap with Fannie; Sam on a sleeping mat close to Daisy, a blanket pulled over his shoulders. His face was still so pale, but at least he wasn't wet with sweat anymore.

"She's the only thing that keeps me going," Daisy admitted. "Her and Sam."

Nell looked up at her. "Different fathers?" she asked curiously, without judgment.

"And mothers." Daisy smiled. "Sam isn't mine. He just came up to me one night, and I couldn't turn him away."

Nell gazed at her. "Why, Daisy, one would never imagine he wasn't yours, the way you love him." She bumped her shoulder amiably against Daisy's. "There aren't many like you about. That's why Fannie's so special."

"I don't know." Daisy sighed. "I've always struggled so much."

"It's the struggle that makes us great sometimes," said Nell.

It was good to be here with Nell, Daisy thought, even if a cold wind blasted through the drafty gaps in the walls and made the fire sputter from time to time. Even Mr. Patrick was kind in his way; he sat across from them, engrossed in whittling a piece of wood with an old, blunt knife.

"I just hope one day the struggle will be over," she murmured.

"It will," said Nell. "One way or another."

Before Daisy could ask what she meant, a soft voice spoke beside her. "Mama Daisy?"

Her heart flipped over, and she turned to see Sam looking up at her, his brown eyes bright and interested.

"Sammy, darling." Daisy almost fell over herself to get to him. She reached out and touched his forehead, and it was gloriously cool, a thin sheen of sweat touching her skin. "Oh, darling," she cried, bending down to hug him.

"I'm hungry," he whispered.

"Nell, he's better." Daisy sat up, tears wet on her cheeks, and pulled the child into her lap. "He's so much better."

Sam leaned his little head against her chest. Nell's eyes were shining. "I saved some bread," she said, laughing with relief. "Would you like some bread, Sam?"

He looked at her in confusion, then relaxed against Daisy again. "Yes, please."

Nell hastened off to get the bread, and Daisy cuddled the boy close, kissing his forehead over and over. "I'm so glad you're better, darling," she whispered. "I love you so much."

Sam snuggled his head against her. "I love you too, Mama Daisy," he whispered.

And for Daisy, that was reason enough to continue with the struggle for a thousand years.

PART IV

CHAPTER 11

One Year Later

Jack knelt down on the floor beside the bed, ignoring the faint smell from the enamel chamber pot beneath it. He set Mr. Tanner's shoes out in front of him, pulling the tongue wide, loosening the laces, then reached up to take a pair of long striped stockings from where they lay on the bed. Mr. Tanner's feet were cold to the touch; Jack made haste to pull the stockings over them, then took one in each of his hands. They were so small and bony and frail in his grip, and he chafed them both gently.

"No need for that, lad," wheezed Mr. Tanner. "They'll warm up."

"No point putting shoes on cold feet, Mr. Tanner," said Jack lightly. He knew that the old man didn't like a fuss. Once the feet seemed a little warmer, he tugged the shoes over them and laced them up neatly, then tidied up Mr. Tanner's trouser legs around them.

"Thank you," grunted Mr. Tanner, with obvious embarrassment.

Jack wished that the old man wouldn't seem so embarrassed around him. After all, what he was doing was a pale thing compared to the love and kindness Mr. Tanner had shown him after his accident. Putting on a pair of shoes, making a bed, emptying a chamber pot – these were all small things compared to the weeks of washing and feeding and dressing that Mr. Tanner had done for Jack.

"Ready to go down?" Jack asked.

Mr. Tanner nodded, and Jack held out an arm. The old man rose stiffly and kept a hand on Jack's arm as they headed out of the tiny flat above the cobbler's shop; it consisted of little more than a bed pushed against the wall, a table against the opposite window, a coal stove, a chair, and a few cupboards. Jack's sleeping mat was rolled up and propped neatly against the corner, and there was a tiny washroom through the door to the left.

They took the door to the right now, heading down a staircase and into the shop, which smelled of fresh leather. Mr. Tanner let go of Jack's arm and tottered over to the stool behind the counter, upon which he clambered laboriously, gripping the counter for support. Jack seized a straw broom and whisked it across the floor, sweeping a little dust out of the front door and flipping the sign behind the glass to "OPEN".

Mr. Tanner was paging through a ledger on the countertop. "Are Mrs. Boswick's shoes ready for her?"

"Yes, sir," said Jack. "They're under the counter."

Mr. Tanner peered at them. "So they are. And you'll be repairing those boots for young Johnny Harding today?"

"I will, sir. I've already cut the new soles. I just have to put them on."

"Good lad." Mr. Tanner made a note in the ledger. He sighed, looking up at Jack. "Now what would I do without you?"

"What would *I* do without you, sir?" Jack smiled at him. "I would be dead, that's what."

"You should know that you owe me no debt for that," said Mr. Tanner quietly. "I don't hold you to it."

"Sir, but I owe you my life."

"And I owe you mine, son, and my business besides. I could never have kept this place going over the past year or so without you. These old hands..." Mr. Tanner sadly raised his twisted hands, the fingers swollen and misshapen with rheumatism. "I'm no good for anything anymore."

"That's nonsense, sir, respectfully."

Mr. Tanner laughed. "Respectfully." He shook his head. "Well, lad, you're a good cobbler in your own right now. You don't have to stay here with some old codger. You could even start up a shop of your own in some other part of the city, somewhere more glamorous than this, where people will pay you more than the mere pittance these miserly souls care to give me."

"I couldn't leave you, sir."

Mr. Tanner cocked his head slightly to one side. "And what about your dreams of finding pretty Daisy Parker, then?"

The mention of Daisy's name sent a familiar agony of thrill, loss, and longing through Jack's body. He leaned against the counter, his head hanging, a great mist of sorrow descending upon him.

"I'm sorry, lad," said Mr. Tanner, seeing his face. "I didn't mean..."

"No, sir, it's not you." Jack sighed. "Three years I've been searching for Daisy, and I've searched all over this city. I even found her handcart... and why would she be parted from it?" He held back the lump in his throat. "She's gone, sir. I know she is."

Mr. Tanner gave him a long, contemplative look. "Yet on a Sunday afternoon, you still walk the streets looking for her."

Jack dropped his eyes. "I should stop, I know."

"That's not what I was going to say, lad." Mr. Tanner's eyes grew misty. "I was in love once too, you know."

Jack looked up at him, surprised. Mr. Tanner had never talked about a woman before; Jack had always assumed he was a lifelong bachelor.

"Don't look so startled." Mr. Tanner chuckled wryly. "I have a heart, lad. And bonny young Frederica Jones, well, she stole that heart right away. Died giving birth to our first child, poor lass. Took the little one with her." He sighed, a deep and unhealed sorrow sketched briefly across his face.

"I'm sorry, Mr. Tanner," said Jack. "I didn't know."

"I don't speak of it, lad. Not much to say about it." Mr. Tanner cleared his throat and looked down at his hands, pulling a pair of shoes due to be repaired out from under the counter and toying with them as if to give himself something to do. "But this I do know: I would have searched for Frederica for three years, too. That love is the best thing my life ever had in it. It isn't something to give up on lightly."

Jack blinked away the surge of tears threatening at the corners of his eyes.

"Daisy is your Frederica," said Mr. Tanner. "Don't stop looking, Jack. You'll find her someday."

SHRIEKS AND GIGGLES of excitement filled the little tenement. Fannie, Sam, Delia and Franklin were running mad laps around the puny room, circumnavigating its meagre furnishings: the stove in one corner, the three sleeping pallets, the table made of two barrels and some planks, the trunk that contained all the worldly possessions of the Parker and O'Leary families. One of them knocked briefly against Daisy's calves, almost making her spill some of the gruel she was tipping carefully into the bowls on the table.

"Children!" Nell scolded, lifting the kettle from the stove to make tea. "Stop that at once!"

Franklin stopped in his tracks. Delia slammed into him, and they tumbled over into a merry heap on the ground, Fannie bouncing after them. Sam, however, came to a tidy halt and looked up at Nell with his huge, soft eyes.

"I'm sorry, Mrs. O'Leary," he said. "We're a bit excited."

Daisy couldn't help smiling at the well-spoken seven-year-old, and she saw Nell's stern exterior melting instantly. "Don't you worry, pet." She chucked Sam fondly under the chin. "You have reason to be."

"I'm excited, too, I have to admit," said Daisy, scraping the last drops of gruel from the pot. "But I'll miss you all terribly."

"Oh, Daisy!" Nell laughed. "We'll be right down the hall, you know. You're only moving to the tenement on the end of the hallway, not to Africa."

Daisy grinned. "I can't wait to have my own tenement. I've been hoping for this moment since… well, since everything went wrong."

Nell gave her a sympathetic smile, patting her on the shoulder. "You're doing well for yourself, Daisy. Bart would be very proud."

Daisy lowered her head, blinking back her tears, and looked over at where Fannie was playing more quietly with Delia. Her little girl had colour in her cheeks again; her red-gold hair was rich and shining, the way it had been four years ago when they had first lost everything. Now, finally, Daisy was gaining back some ground.

She moved her hips slightly side to side to feel the reassuring tug of the weight of coins she had sewn into her hem. It was more than enough to pay the first week's rent, and tonight, she and her children would be moving into the newly vacated tenement. They would have a home all their own.

It was going to be wonderful.

Mr. Patrick sat down at the table, on the single chair, reserved as usual for him. "Now all you need is a good little husband, Daisy," he said, "and you'll have it all."

Daisy laughed. "Someday," she said.

She thought again of Jack, of the way he had so narrowly slipped through her fingers, and offered up a humble prayer. *You've provided so much for me, Lord. Our situation is so much better.*

But oh, if You would bring Jack back... Please, it would make my heart whole again.

It was worth a try, she thought. She had prayed and prayed for the tenement, and now it was finally happening. Maybe her dream of finding Jack would come true, as well.

THE MARKETPLACE WAS a perfect spot for singing, and it was largely responsible for the newfound prosperity that had come to the Parkers and O'Learys. Nell had stumbled upon it one day shortly after they had been driven from the condemned building a few months ago. It was just a few blocks from the slum where their tenement was located, yet the moment Daisy stepped into the square, it was as though the sun shone a little brighter. There was a church on the corner of the square, and the rest of it was lined with shops, rows of peddlers gathering with their stalls and carts in the centre.

Somehow, impossibly, this had become a place where the rich and poor worked together. Daisy wasn't sure how that could be, but the people moving through this square seemed to come from all walks of life: some in rich and gaudy clothes, others in rags, all of them buying and selling from one another. As a result, she had watched over the past few months as the poorest peddlers grew slowly a little richer, wore slightly better clothes, put new wheels on their handcarts.

And got their own tenements.

The thought of sleeping in a room all their own thrilled her as she took up her usual spot under the streetlamp outside the bakery, whose owner never chased her off; he sometimes gave her stale bread, for free, saying that he liked her singing. She didn't know why people here were so kind, but she thought perhaps the rosy-cheeked, smiling minister of the little white church had something to do with it. He always gave her money when he walked past even though his own clothes were a little on the shabby side.

The children took up their places without being told, and Daisy leaned against the pole, starting her first song.

"Our God is a good God, He reigns in the Heavens," she sang, easily remembering the words she'd overheard an elderly woman sing repeatedly in the workhouse so many years ago. "He reigns with such love – our God is a good God."

A smiling, round-faced woman paused to listen to the whole hymn, closing her eyes and mouthing the words alongside Daisy. Passing by, another man tossed a sixpence to Fannie, who clenched her fingers around it and squirrelled it away.

Daisy felt a sudden pang of nervousness, losing pitch for a single note. She corrected the stumble quickly, glancing at the round-faced woman, who didn't seem to have noticed. Why, then, was Daisy suddenly feeling so fearful? She wanted to look around, but she had also spied the golden clasp of the woman's purse, and she had to finish the hymn well if the woman was going to give her something.

Fighting the urge to turn around, feeling as though something dark was creeping up on her, Daisy sang valiantly to the end. There was an alley behind her, and she had a dreadful feeling that someone was standing in the mouth of it. Someone armed. The memory of the thugs who had tried to take Fannie and the boys who had given her the scar on her arm crowded closely around her.

Finally, the hymn was finished, and Daisy was breathless. Wet-eyed, the woman applauded. "So beautiful!" she cried. "God bless you, darling."

Daisy longed to spin around, but she forced a smile. "Thank you," she said. "Oh, thank you!"

The woman had dropped an entire shilling into Sam's hand, and a few pennies in Fannie's for good measure. The two children might not have known anything about arithmetic, but they were well versed in the despairing mathematics of currency and poverty, and they both cheered.

Daisy held on until the woman had turned to leave, then whipped around, sucking in a breath. But the alley was completely empty.

There was no one there.

A RESTLESS WIND gusted around the square, and Daisy glanced longingly at the great clock on the church tower. A quarter past twelve. How was it possible? She felt as though she'd been here all day, and it wasn't the wind that was making goosebumps rise on her arms.

She rubbed at them, trying to get them to go away.

"Are you cold, Mama Daisy?" Sam asked, looking up at her. His mouth was scattered with crumbs from the sticky buns Daisy had bought for him and Fannie for lunch – a special treat to celebrate the new tenement.

"No, no. I'm fine," said Daisy, smiling.

"You shivered," Fannie pointed out.

"I'm not cold," said Daisy. "It's just..." She glanced around again, her eyes on the alleyway, wishing that evening would come, and she could go to the safety of her tenement. But the feeling in the pit of her belly wasn't excitement. It was fear.

What did she have to be afraid of? No one had ever harmed her here. So why did it feel like something dark was stalking her?

"Can we go back to our new tenement now?" Fannie asked.

"No, darling. Not yet." Daisy sighed, regretting the sticky buns. "We still need to make enough money for supper."

It seemed to take ages. Daisy struggled to hold her notes; her singing was losing its usual, ethereal quality, and people passed her by without a second glance. The more she tried to concentrate on the songs, the more she kept glancing around, expecting something horrible to happen at any second. If it wasn't for the regulars who tossed them a few coins out of pity, Daisy would never have made enough money for supper.

As it was, darkness was falling rapidly by the time Daisy had been able to buy a packet of root vegetables to make soup for supper. She gave the packet to Sam, who carried it tightly with one arm, and took both of the children's hands to keep them close. The streets were bustling, and the spring evening was growing cold.

"Come on," she said, with a sense of deep relief spreading through her. "Let's get home – to *our* home, this time."

"Hooray!" Fannie cheered, and Sam permitted himself a wide smile.

Daisy hastened out of the square and followed the twisting, cobbled streets toward the slum. She tried to think of the cozy tenement waiting for her, of having a space all her own, but it seemed as though the shadows were closing in on her. Darting from one pool of streetlight to the other, she took hurried breaths, clinging tightly to the hands of the children.

"Mama, I'm tired," Fannie complained. "Why are we going so fast?"

"Yes, answer the child," purred a voice behind her. "Where are you going in such a hurry?"

It was a masculine voice, deep and gruff and slightly inebriated, and it made Daisy break immediately into a run. But a second later, the silhouettes of two men appeared at the end of the narrow street down which she was moving. She stumbled to a halt, whipped around. Another man blocked the other side of the street.

The buildings on either side of her were businesses, closed and shuttered for the night, and the rumble of traffic on the nearby road drowned out any chance of a scream. Daisy was shaking to the marrow of her bones.

"Please." Her voice was both desperate and despairing. "Please, don't harm my children."

Fannie's small hand was trembling in hers. "Mama? Mama, who are they?"

All three men were advancing, and Daisy felt tears of terror running down her cheeks as they stepped into the light of the lone streetlamp nearby, and she saw the expression in their eyes. It was worse than malice or fury.

It was lust.

"Don't worry," one of them chuckled. "It's you we're after."

She redoubled her grip on the hands of the children and turned toward the lone man, even turning her back on the other two felt like exposing herself to oncoming cannonballs. Rage and terror burned in her chest like bile, and she knew she had only this second in which to act.

So she acted. She bolted forward, yanking the children with her, letting out a scream of fear and determination as she ran, throwing herself toward the gap between the wall and the man. He lunged after her; she dodged, anticipating it, and shouldered her way past him toward freedom and the street and light and –

His hand slammed shut around her elbow like a shackle, and as he yanked her back, Daisy had the presence of mind to open her hands and let the children go. Pulled forward by their own momentum, they staggered on at a run as the man threw both arms around Daisy and hauled her back with a force that lifted her off her feet.

"Run!" Daisy screamed at them. "Run home! Run, run!"

"Mama!" shrieked Fannie. "*Mama*!"

Daisy was helpless, her feet kicking in the air, the man's arms an iron grip around her. She screamed again, and then she was being flung to the ground, terror lurching in her belly for a moment before she landed on her back with a force that knocked the air from her lungs, her head thudding agonisingly against the stone. Dark stars popped in front of her eyes, and there were loud shouts around her, hot breath panting in her face. The first man was pinning her to the ground with his hands on her shoulders. *Shoulders*!

As her spinning head began to clear, Daisy realised that her hands were free. She raised them and clawed at the man's face, at his eyes. He lurched back with a shriek, and Daisy lunged to sit up, but another set of hands was grabbing her around the throat and ramming her head back against the stone.

"Mama!" Fannie screamed.

Their intentions were unmistakable. One of them was fumbling with the front of her dress; Daisy heard a grunt, then the rip of fabric, cool air where she didn't want air to be. Fannie couldn't see this. Fannie would never forget it.

"Fannie, run!" Daisy shouted.

"Shut up!" roared the voice of the first man, the one whose face she had clawed. He shoved aside the man busy with her chest and slapped her, the pain was minor compared with the thudding in her head.

His weight was on her, crushing her, and he was grabbing at the hem of her dress, his finger scraping painfully across her shins, and –

Chink, chink.

All three men froze. Daisy was sobbing, hopeless and in agony.

"What's this, then?" growled the first.

The others were tugging at her hem; with the sound of a ripping seam, one of them gasped, then chuckled. “Money!” he said. “Stupid wench sewed her money into her dress!”

“Yes, yes!” roared the first man, and then they were ripping at her dress, tearing it, money scattering, her hard-earned life savings, her chance at a tenement of her own. No one was crushing her now and Daisy somehow managed to sit up despite the way her head spun and the nausea lurching in her stomach.

“No! Please!” she cried. “Please!”

“Silence!” roared one of the men, drawing back a hobnailed boot. When the toe drove into her ribs with a sickening crack, darkness overwhelmed Daisy’s world.

THERE WAS SOBBING, and small hands were touching her face, shaking her shoulder. “Mama... Mama!”

Daisy groaned, agony flooding her every fibre. She wanted to move, to sit up and put her arms around the two crying children, but pain blossomed through her entire body, and she could do nothing more than groan again.

“Please, Mama Daisy, wake up.” Sam was tugging at her sleeve the way he had done under the bridge all those years ago. “Wake up.”

Daisy groaned, then coughed, and the movement felt as though someone was thrusting a knife through her ribs. She rolled onto her side, hugging herself and sobbing. She was freezing cold; she could feel the air on her bare legs, but to her utter relief, it seemed that her undergarments were still in place. Still, they had ripped the skirt of her dress to pieces. The money was all gone.

"Mama?" Fannie whimpered.

Her child's voice held such desolation that Daisy managed to pry her eyes open, although one was so swollen that it would barely admit more than a slit of light. It was terribly dark. Fannie's face was red with crying, and she clutched one of Daisy's hands in both of hers.

"It's all right," Daisy croaked out, then coughed again, unable to stop herself from sobbing with the pain. "Mama's all right."

"You're hurt, Mama," sobbed Fannie.

"Mama will be all right," Daisy whispered, closing her eyes again and taking the deepest, slowest breaths she could against the pain. She was far from alright. Her body throbbed with pain, and her money was gone, and her hope was shattered.

But for the sake of Sam and Fannie, she couldn't give up, even at this lowest of all moments.

IT TOOK Daisy more than an hour before she was able to sit up, trembling and hugging her wounded ribs with one arm. Even with that meagre support, her ribs ached like nothing she had ever known before in her life.

Sam and Fannie, bless their little souls, tried to help her where they could. When she tried to rise, Fannie grabbed her free hand and pulled, and Sam braced himself against her back and pushed, and somehow, she staggered to her feet even though the ground felt as though it was pitching madly beneath her. She put out a hand, and Sam and Fannie both grabbed it, steadying her.

"Are we going home, Mama?" Fannie asked in a whisper.

Home. They didn't have a home anymore. Not now that Daisy didn't have the money for the tenement. Nell and Mr. Patrick already had chosen new tenants to share their rent; Daisy could only hope they hadn't moved in yet.

"Yes," she croaked. "We're going home, darling." She was uncertain where it was, but Fannie and Sam seemed to understand, and grasped her hand to lead her very slowly through the muddy streets.

The walk had taken ten minutes in the bright sunshine of that morning. Now, it seemed to be an eternity, every step another burst of agony, every breath burning in her lungs. Several times she had to stop and breathe for a few minutes so that her swimming vision would clear; twice she stopped and vomited in the gutter, torturous with her aching ribs.

Finally, finally, they had reached the tenement, and they were plodding up the stairs, Sam pushing and Fannie pulling. When they reached the top of the hallway, Fannie's admirable nerve finally failed her. She let go of Daisy's hand and ran toward the O'Learys tenement, hammering madly on the door.

"Nell, Nell!" she sobbed out. "Help. Help!"

The door swung open at once, and Nell stepped onto the threshold, wide-eyed. "Fannie! What's – " Her eyes found Daisy and she froze. "Oh, Daisy."

"Help me," Daisy croaked.

Nell rushed to her, grasping her arm and pulling it over her shoulders. "Daisy, darling, what happened? Your dress is torn all to pieces." A dreadful look came over her face. "Were you – "

"Some men attacked. They tried. But they took my money and ran away." Daisy ground the words out between gritted teeth. "Please, Nell, can I stay with you tonight?"

"Oh, Daisy, I'm so sorry." Nell's voice broke. "All that money..."

"Gone," said Daisy. "All gone. Please."

Fannie had disappeared into the tenement. She popped out into the hallway again now, her face a mask of confusion. "Mama, there's other people here," she said.

"I'm sorry, Daisy," said Nell. "The other family, the Connors... they've already moved in."

Daisy didn't mean for a sob to escape her, but it did. All she wanted now was Nell's kinship and a place to sleep, but she knew that the empty tenement was locked, that the landlord would throw her out forever if he caught her inside it without having received the rent. She had nowhere to go.

"What's going on?" Mr. Patrick's voice demanded, and he appeared in the doorway. His face fell. "Daisy!"

"She was attacked, Papa," said Nell. "Her money was all stolen. She... she has nowhere to go."

Mr. Patrick glanced into the tenement, then back at Daisy. "Well, she'll have to stay here tonight."

"Do we have space?" Nell asked hesitantly.

Mr. Patrick reached out and took Daisy's arm, steadying her.

"For Daisy, we will always have space," he said.

CHAPTER 12

Mr. Patrick's sentiment had been generous, but truth be told, the tenement simply didn't have the room for three families to fit inside.

Daisy lay very still, gritting her teeth against her pain. She lay on her wounded side; while her torn skin cried out in pain at the pressure, it was the only way she felt able to breathe. She pillowed her head on one arm, the other tight against her chest. Her heart yearned to hold Fannie, as she usually did, but the child was sandwiched so close against Daisy's chest, and Nell so tightly against Fannie, that there just wasn't space.

The sleeping pallet had been cramped enough already with Fannie, Sam, and Daisy on it. Now, Nell had joined them, and they were crammed together like sardines in a tin. Mr. Patrick was sharing his pallet with Delia, Franklin, and one of the boys from the new family, the Connors; they themselves slept on the third pallet with three of their other boys. Everyone was being crushed.

And Daisy couldn't sleep a single wink, not with the pain in her head and ribs.

She squeezed her eyes shut, tears escaping down her cheeks. *Why are you doing this, Lord?* she prayed in agony. *Just this morning I had a tenement. I prayed for You to send me Jack. Was I ungrateful? Is that why You've done this to me?*

No response came. The night stretched long and black before her, and Daisy buried her face in Fannie's back and wept.

MORNING CAME after a meagre half-hour of sleep snatched out of the jaws of pain. When she woke, Daisy felt even worse. Every muscle in her body pounded steadily with pain. She sat up with a long moan, realizing with a jolt that sunlight shone inside the room.

"Fannie?" she cried out nervously. "Sam?"

"Right here, Mama," said Fannie. She was sitting by the table, nibbling on a tiny, hard rusk.

"I'm sorry. It's all I had to give her," said Nell apologetically. She was pouring a tin mug of tea. "Come and drink your tea."

"Nell, you've been so kind." Daisy sat up with a moan, then struggled to her feet. Her stomach lurched with nausea, and she could barely stand even the smell of the tea. "I… I should go."

"Where are you going to go?" asked Nell, sorrow in her eyes.

Daisy knew that no one could tolerate another night like last night. No one had slept well, and if Daisy couldn't pay half the O'Learys rent, then the Connors would have to stay. She needed to make money. She could only see her way forward if she had money.

"I don't know yet," she said. "I'll go down to the square…"

"Daisy, your dress," said Nell softly.

Daisy looked down at it. The skirt hung just past her knees in sad tatters.

"It'll have to do," she said, but she wasn't sure she would even be allowed to stand on her usual corner and sing. She was certain no one would give her money. But what else could she do? Perhaps the kind baker or the minister would do something for her. The O'Learys would if they could, she knew, but they just didn't have anything to give.

There was nothing else for it. Daisy took the hands of the children and led them out of the tenement. This time, she couldn't seem to pray.

RAIN PATTERED ON THE SQUARE, washing filth down the gutter past the children where they knelt on the pavement. Both of them were chewing on pieces of bread; the kindly baker had given them the bread, and given Daisy a couple of old flour sacks, which she had hastily fashioned into a sort of covering. It wasn't a real skirt, but at least her undergarments where no longer showing.

She was grateful to the baker, but it hadn't helped much. Her voice was feeble and broken; she was struggling to remember the lyrics, and her songs all fell flat.

"Hold Thy Cross before my closing eyes," she sang, fumbling the notes. "Shine through the gloom, and..." She faltered. She'd sung this hymn so many times before. Why couldn't she remember it now? A man who had been listening turned away, shaking his head, and Daisy's eyes burned with tears. He wasn't going to give her any money.

No one had given her money all day, and it was well past noon. If she didn't make anything soon, she would have nowhere to go tonight, and they would be back on the streets. No cart to sleep under. Nowhere to go.

The thought sucked at her feet, a great abyss of pure terror.

Clearing her throat, she tried again, picking the song that she knew better than she knew her own soul. "Hush, little baby, don't say a word. Mama's going to buy you a mockingbird..."

She had laboured halfway through the lullaby when the man walked up to her and stopped, listening. He was short and stout, with only one eye, a patch over the other; when he grinned, gold flashed in his teeth. Something about him made nervousness prickle over Daisy's arms, but she kept singing, and Fannie and Sam directed their pitiful gazes toward him. Hope grew slowly in Daisy's heart. The man was wearing two golden rings. If he could only throw a shilling her way, she was sure she could find a place to sleep for the night. Just long enough to regain a few shreds of her courage.

She finished the lullaby as strongly as she could, panting with pain and effort, her ribs stinging with each breath. The man stepped forward. Fannie and Sam stretched out their hands, but he ignored them.

"You know," he said, "a woman of your talents shouldn't be singin' on the streets."

Daisy stared at him, at the way his eyes roved across her body, then found her face again and grinned.

"I beg your pardon, sir?" she said.

"Singin' for your supper – now, is that any way for a pretty girl to live?" The man stepped forward, holding out a hand. Daisy flinched away from it, and he chortled. "Skittish, are you? Well, don't worry. I'm not here to hurt you. I want to help you."

"You do?" said Daisy nervously.

"Yes. I'm looking for girls just like you – girls who want to work." He raised an eyebrow. "And I'm offering good money, too. Room, board, and a shilling each day."

A shilling each day – and room and board! Daisy didn't know what she would do with all of that money. Her breath was snatched from her.

"We'll do something for the brats, too," the man added, glancing at Fannie and Sam.

"What kind of work?" Daisy asked. "Where?"

"I'll show you." The man offered his hand again. "You just have to give me a little trust, that's all."

Daisy glanced at his hand, then back at his face.

"A warm room for the night – now doesn't that sound good? With all the food you can eat. Meat, too. Three times a day," the man cajoled.

Daisy didn't like the feeling he was giving her, but his offering sounded like heaven. In despair, she looked down at the children, and remembered the time when Sam had been ill. How close she had come to losing him. If it was still raining tonight, and they slept in some alleyway, would his chest fail him again? Would she be able to save him this time?

Would she be able to save Fannie? She thought of what Bart would think of her, how she had lost everything, how her daughter was back on the street.

"Come along then," said the man.

Daisy took a deep breath. She had no choice. She had to go with this man. She stepped forward, and that was when she heard the voice.

"Daisy! Daisy, it's you!"

Daisy's breath froze in her chest. The voice came from somewhere to her right, near the church, and she knew it. She had heard it in her dreams a thousand times. But surely... surely this wasn't happening. Surely God would not answer her prayers now, not after how she had raged at Him last night. She was imagining it. She was delirious.

Fannie looked up. "Mama, did you hear that?"

"Daisy!" The voice was closer this time.

"Jack!" Fannie jumped to her feet and ran off with the abandon of a small child. "Jack!"

Daisy allowed herself, finally, to turn around, and Jack was bending down with his arms outstretched and his wonderful grey eyes dancing, and when Fannie reached him, he scooped her into his arms and spun her around, looking at her as though she was a perfect princess. Looking at her just the way Bart always had. When Daisy saw them together like that, she could feel Bart smiling down from heaven.

She couldn't move, couldn't breathe, only stared as Jack lowered Fannie to the ground and kissed the top of her head. "My, how you've grown," he gasped. "You're so beautiful."

"Mama, look." Fannie was clinging to Jack's hand. "It's Jack. It's really Jack."

Jack looked up at her, and his grey eyes widened. But somehow, they didn't see her sackcloth skirt or her bruised face. They met her gaze, and they were filled with love, deep and calm and slow and steady, and he strode toward her quickly.

"Jack..." Daisy breathed.

"Excuse me?" The man was still standing there; Daisy had forgotten he existed. "I've made you an offer, woman. You need to accept it."

Jack's eyes raked the short man, and he reached out and gripped Daisy's arm, firmly and gently. "Daisy is coming with me," he said sharply.

The man sneered, and his hands bunched into fists by his sides. For an instant, Daisy feared he might start a fight. He glared up into Jack's face and read something there that made him hesitate.

"Fool," he spat instead, and strode away.

Jack let go of her arm, a smile spreading across his features as he stared into her eyes. "Oh, Daisy, I'm so glad I found you," he breathed. "I've been looking everywhere for you."

"You've been – looking?" Daisy breathed.

"I... I have." He hesitated, shyness in his eyes.

"Jack... it's been three years." She searched his face, a wild hope beating within her chest. Could it be? Could it be that he felt the same thing for her that she felt for him, that she had continued to feel for him all this time? The thing that was flaring wildly within her at the sight of him now?

"I know... I..." Jack cleared his throat. "I had to find you."

A small hand closed over Daisy's fingers. "Mama Daisy?" said Sam, nervously.

"Oh!" Daisy blinked, looking down at the boy. "Sam, darling, this is Jack."

"Jack," squealed Fannie happily, throwing her arms around his legs.

"Who's this?" Jack asked.

"This is my little Sam." Daisy ran a hand through his hair. "I... well, he's part of my family now."

"It's good to meet you, Sam." Jack smiled at him, warmth in his eyes, and every corner of Daisy melted at the sight of his instant love for the boy. Then he turned suddenly to Daisy, reaching for the strap of the leather satchel over his shoulder. "I have these for you," he said, unhooking it and holding it out to her.

Daisy took the satchel and flipped it open, and what she saw inside made her heart turn over. Books. She lifted them out of the satchel, and there was no doubt. They were neatly glued, their spines sturdy, their pages rustling easily under her hands. They were her books, the ones she had not been able to glue. The ones that Jack had taken and promised to repair for her.

Three years ago.

"All these years," Daisy breathed. She raised her face to stare up at Jack, feeling hope dance upon her lips as a smile. "All these years, and you still kept them."

"I made you a promise, Daisy," said Jack. "I would never break a promise to you."

She saw the truth in his eyes, and she held the books close to her chest. Her heart wanted to stay here, in this moment, gazing up at him, for a thousand years. But her hunger and fear prevailed. She knew she had to feed the children and find them a home, and she had to do it quickly, before darkness fell.

"Do you know where I can sell them?" she managed, in a small and quavering voice.

"Daisy..." Jack paused. "Things have changed for me. A lot of things."

She stared at him. He was right; she had never seen him looking like this before, and good health made him all the more splendid. His eyes shone. His black hair was neatly trimmed and combed over his forehead in a glossy wing, and there was colour in his face, straightness in his spine, no longer the stooped look of one living out of a handcart and sleeping on hard earth.

"I'm happy for you," Daisy whispered.

"You don't understand." Jack reached out then, his fingers wrapping hesitantly around hers. The warmth of his touch sent goosebumps skittering across her frame. "I want to make things better for you, too. I want you..." He sucked in a breath. "I want you to come with me."

"Do you have a tenement, Jack?" asked Fannie in her small voice.

"Better. I have a room. I have a good job, and hope, and a future, and even a kind of family." Jack was staring at Daisy, his eyes begging her to understand. "But not yet the family I've always wanted."

Daisy's breath hitched in her chest. His hand squeezed hers lightly, answering her question, telling her that she was not the only one who felt a bright candle burning deep within her soul.

Jack looked down, running his free hand over Fannie's head, ruffling Sam's hair. When his gaze returned to hers, he was almost crying.

"Say something," he breathed.

"I don't know what to say," said Daisy. She hugged the books tighter. "I... I feel I've been waiting for you all this time."

"I have a home," Jack repeated. "A good, warm room, with space enough for you and the children, and an old man who treats me like a son, a man who told me just days ago not to give up on finding you." He squeezed her hand again. "Oh, Daisy, say that you'll come with me. Say that you'll come to stay and make me the happiest man in the world, for I have loved you since I first saw you."

She was being offered a home. Food. Warmth and safety. Daisy's eyes stung uncontrollably at the thought. "Jack... I... I need you. I would love to."

He gave her a long, searching look. "There's only one bit of difficulty."

Her heart swooped. "What's that?"

"Well, there's only really one room big enough." Jack cleared his throat. "I can't take you home unless... unless you marry me."

Daisy's heart skipped. Was he proposing? When he looked up at her, she saw the question in his soft grey eyes. And there was only one way she could answer it. She did as she had longed to do for so many years. She threw her arms around his neck and kissed him.

There was only a tiny handful of people in the small white church, each more ragged than the next. The only well-dressed man was the minister in his neat suit, a rose cut from the garden in his buttonhole; Jack wore a matching rose in the lapel of his worn tweed coat. Then there was Fannie and Sam, watching with wide, adoring eyes from the nearest pew, Delia and Franklin sitting beside them. And beside Jack stood Mr. O'Leary and Mr. Tanner; and beside Daisy stood Nell, with shining eyes.

Daisy stood in her sackcloth wedding gown and gazed into the soft eyes of the second love of her life. She barely heard the minister's words. All she could hear was the symphony of joy in her heart, a wordless paean of her soul.

Her prayers had all been answered. Not always the way she had expected, but sometimes in ways that had been even better.

"I do," Jack was saying. And then it was Daisy's turn to say, "I do." And finally, Jack slipped an iron ring onto her finger, and she put a similar one on his; and then he kissed her, and she was Mrs. Jack Honor, and in that moment, the flawed and broken world was absolutely perfect.

They walked out of the church hand-in-hand; Fannie walking beside Daisy, Sam beside Jack. A family in every way that really mattered. She felt tears stinging her eyes at the richness of this blessing – one far greater than any of the material things she had so sorely lacked – and also with a hint of sorrow. On her first wedding day, she had never dreamed there would be a second. With a pang of grief, coming as it always did at an inopportune moment, she suddenly missed Bart more than she could express.

Fannie gasped beside her. “Mama,” she cried. “Bird!”

They all stopped, looking up at the sky. “Why,” said Jack, “it’s a gull.”

The seagull swooped down and perched for a moment on the church wall right in front of them. It cocked its head a little to one side, and for a moment, Daisy looked into its eyes. They were warmly amber, and there was something friendly in them. Their gazes locked for only an instant before the bird spread its wings and swooped away, leaving behind a single, white feather.

It was only a seagull ... but in Daisy’s eyes, it might as well have been a bird of paradise.

The End

CONTINUE READING...

THANK you for reading ***The Peddler's Widow!*** **Are you wondering what to read next?** Why not read ***An Orphan Called Christmas?*** **Here's a sneak peek for you:**

Beulah Ellis reminded herself that she had done this before. It wasn't easy, not with Dovie's screams of pain and panic echoing around the room. The little girl lay in a tangle of sweat-soaked sheets in the room that had once belonged to her mother, decades ago, and her shrieks threatened to lift the roof from the cottage.

"It's all right, pet. It's all right." Beulah smoothed sweaty hair back from Dovie's face with one hand, gripping the girl's hand in the other.

Dovie fell back against her pillows, gasping, her body trembling violently, her hand clasped over the swollen curve of her abdomen. "What's happening, Granny?" she gasped.

Beulah looked into Dovie's wide, milky-blue eyes. Fifteen years old. She was just a bairn herself, but like it or not, she and Beulah would be bringing a child into the world this night. Beulah could only pray that the baby's mother, a child herself, would survive it.

She wondered how to explain. How to tell Dovie that what she might have believed was innocent, forbidden fun with that handsome lad who worked in her parents' garden had led to this. Had Carol never discussed such things with her daughter?

Before Beulah could answer, another shriek tore from Dovie's lungs. The girl's body folded, doubling with the force of the contraction, her knees drawing up, her scream growing louder and louder and reaching a desperate pitch as her skinny legs curled in pain.

"Hush, hush," Beulah soothed, stroking Dovie's forehead as the girl's trembling grip crushed the little bones in Beulah's hand.

"What's *happening*?" Dovie screamed.

Beulah pulled back Dovie's skirt, saw the purplish crown of the baby beginning to emerge.

"You're having your baby, just like we said," she told her.

"Right now?" Dovie panted, sweat pouring down her cheeks. "*Now*? Why does it hurt so much?"

"Yes. Right now," said Beulah. "Be brave now, pet." She released the girl's hand, took up her position at the bottom of the bed. "And when I tell you to push, do it."

Sobbing, Dovie fell back against her pillows, her tiny body heaving wildly with agony and terror. Outside, Beulah could hear something. Singing. She looked through the window. Sure enough, in the street below this attic that had been Carol's room and was now Dovie's, she could see a string of boys and girls in neat white robes striding down the street. They carried candles that cast golden haloes around them as they walked.

THANKS FOR READING

If you **love Victorian Romance**, **Click Here**

https://victorian.subscribemenow.com/

to hear about all **New Faye Godwin Romance Releases! I will let you know as soon as they become available!**

Thank you, Friends! If you enjoyed ***The Peddler's Widow,*** would you kindly take a couple minutes to leave a positive review on Amazon? It only takes a moment, and positive reviews truly make a difference. Thank you so much! I appreciate it!

Much love,

Faye Godwin

MORE FAYE GODWIN VICTORIAN ROMANCES!

We love rich, dramatic Victorian Romances and have a library of Faye Godwin titles just for you! (Remember that ALL of Faye's Victorian titles can be downloaded FREE with Kindle Unlimited!)

CLICK HERE to discover Faye's Complete Collection of Victorian Romance!

https://ticahousepublishing.com/victorian-romance.html

ABOUT THE AUTHOR

Faye Godwin has been fascinated with Victorian Romance since she was a teen. After reading every Victorian Romance in her public library, she decided to start writing them herself —which she's been doing ever since. Faye lives with her husband and young son in England. She loves to travel throughout her country, dreaming up new plots for her romances. She's delighted to join the Tica House Publishing family and looks forward to getting to know her readers.

contact@ticahousepublishing.com

Printed in Great Britain
by Amazon

22276824R00116